HALL

of

DECEPTION

A POST WWII ROMANTIC SUSPENSE

P.L. JONAS

Black Rose Writing | Texas

ISBN: 978-1-68513-229-3
PUBLISHED BY BLACK ROSE WRITING
www.blackrosewriting.com

Printed in the United States of America
Suggested Retail Price (SRP) $20.95

Hall of Deception is printed in EB Garamond

*As a planet-friendly publisher, Black Rose Writing does its best to eliminate unnecessary waste to reduce paper usage and energy costs, while never compromising the reading experience. As a result, the final word count vs. page count may not meet common expectations.

ACKNOWLEDGEMENTS

This is not my first book nor will it be my last. The people who have stuck with me and the new ones I've met along the way have played a part in developing me as a novelist.

Many thanks to my family, friends, and beta readers who have supported me throughout my writing and publishing journey.

A special thank you to my friend and romance author, Pam Mortensen. Her constant support and feedback as a sounding board, a beta reader, or offering knowledge of the era was a blessing.

Thank you to Amy Craig, a romance author whose expert feedback during the early stages and as a beta reader was very helpful.

And, Reagan Rothe of Black Rose Writing, thank you for selecting this novel for publication and for your timely responses to my many questions. Thank you for bringing me into the BRW family of authors.

HALL

of

DECEPTION

CHAPTER ONE

1953 Massachusetts

I gazed at the massive iron gates towering over my head when sudden panic flooded through me. Did I make a terrible mistake coming here? Turning back to the bus, it pulled away, leaving me in a cloud of exhaust. Resigned, I retrieved the offer letter from my bag and ran my gloved fingers over the embossed letterhead reflecting the same gold gilt crest on the gate.

It read: . . . *offer you the position of tutor . . . arrival at the gated entrance . . . use the call box.* There was a phone box next to the smaller gate. I picked up the receiver and pushed the red button.

A woman's voice answered. "Rothmorton Hall."

"Uh, yes, this is Deirdre, I mean, Dee Danes. I'm expected."

"Wait there. Someone will drive up to get you." The line went dead.

This was it. I could only go forward. I smoothed down my rumpled gray traveling suit, placed the letter in my bag, and pulled out a small mirror. Much to my dismay, several cracks caused pieces to fall out. "That's all I need, seven years of bad luck." Through the slivers, I glimpsed my shoulder-length dark blond hair, frizzy from the coastal humidity. Combing would make it worse. I gave up. When putting the mirror away, my hand touched my most prized possession, a worn copy of *Jane Eyre* by Charlotte Bronte, my favorite book. I fondled the cover and held it to my breast, remembering why I was there.

It was coming true. Ever since I first read it when I was nine, Jane's life spoke to me. She was an ill-treated orphan cast out by family and lived in a horrible orphan's home. I too was an orphan and ill-treated. An elderly cousin took me in until she died when I was fifteen and her daughter, Orpha, did the same. She was civil and not very loving. Another reason I clung to Jane, for she didn't feel loved, and neither did I.

Orpha's spiteful words came back to me. "What a coincidence. Just like your beloved Jane Eyre, running off to a grand estate to tutor a little girl, hoping to find true love. You are obsessed, Dee Dee."

"Not a coincidence, it's fate," I had said with defiance.

When I heard a puttering sound, I peered between the iron bars into the shadows from the tall dense trees and thick bushes. A motorized golf cart with a hard top and open sides appeared, making me step back. The driver was handsome, probably a little older than my twenty-two years, dressed in work pants and a white short-sleeved tee shirt with a pack of cigarettes stuck in one sleeve. He parked and got out, limping to the small gate, and opened it.

"Hello." I adjusted my hat.

"Miss Danes? I'm Ben, the chauffeur. Let me take your bag." His face broke into a friendly grin, lifting the bag it as though it weighed nothing and placed it in the backend.

His friendliness helped me relax, and I returned a smile, sliding into the passenger side and held onto the rail in front. When he got in, he needed to lift his left leg.

"War injury two days before they dropped the bomb." He turned the cart around and drove down the drive.

"I'm sorry. I didn't mean to stare."

"It's okay. Thanks to Mr. Roth, I have this job."

"Did you serve together?"

"Yep, the Navy. The house isn't far. Long trip?" Ben gave me a sidelong glance.

"I must look awful."

"You look great. Don't worry about it. You have those eyes, ya know, Bette Davis eyes. They aren't blue, though. Green?"

I nodded.

"Yeah man, cool." He grinned.

He sure was cute, but his kind of flirtatiousness wasn't for me. A more mature man might fit the bill. "The trip was torture. I'm so glad to be here."

"What the hell?" He slammed on the brakes and I lunged forward, gripping the rail tighter.

Ben went to a tree away from the drive. With a gasp, I nearly fainted at the sight of a large gray cat nailed to the tree. Dead for sure. Its blood had drained down the trunk in long dark squiggles. Ben carefully removed the poor animal from the tree and laid it on the ground.

"I'll come back for it later, after I've dropped you off." When he started to wipe his bloody hands on his pants, I must have made a face and he stopped.

"Here." I thrust out my hanky.

"I got it." Grabbing a rag from the cart, he rubbed his hands clean before getting in.

"Who could have done that?" I shuddered, wondering what I had gotten myself into.

"Don't know. Sorry you had to see that. Your first day and all." He put the cart in gear and we continued on to the house.

I was still shaking when Rothmorton Hall came into view. The horror left my mind temporarily. It was a magnificent example of architecture from the Gilded Age. I hadn't realized such homes existed in America. Three stories of stone with a grand columned entrance.

The cart moved around a circular drive surrounding a large fountain. Water danced in a synchronized pattern up and down, sparkling from the late morning August sunlight. Ben continued to the north side of the house and into an enclosed courtyard.

"The servant's entrance and where I spend most of my day. I live over the garage." He pointed to his left at what appeared to be a former carriage house. Several expensive automobiles sat in open bays, among them a Bentley and a limousine. Ben parked in a spot alongside the house. A mature, short and round woman, in a black dress with a white collar, waved and beamed at us from a doorway leading downstairs.

"She's the housekeeper," he said.

"Thanks." I exited the cart and smiled at the woman.

"Sure thing. Let me know if you need a lift to town. There are bicycles over there, for anyone. To explore the grounds or ride to town."

"Plymouth, right?"

He nodded while taking my bag and left it inside the door.

"Miss Danes, I'm Mrs. Chambers," she said.

I murmured a faint hello as she shook my hand. I followed her down the stairs and through a spacious modern-looking kitchen with shiny stainless-steel counters and overhead lighting. Three men in white uniforms were busy preparing food. She continued on to an office on the other side of the kitchen and waved toward a chair.

I was exhausted and still upset, trying not to plop.

"You look like you've seen a ghost. Would you like some water?" Mrs. Chambers spoke with a slight lilting Irish accent, which went along with her cheerful disposition.

"Please." I took my hanky from my handbag and patted my damp brow.

From a crystal pitcher on a table next to her desk, she poured a glass and handed it to me.

"Bless you," I said. "There . . ." I gulped the water, thirstier than I realized, "was a dead cat nailed to a tree. It was horrible . . . the blood and all." I shuddered again.

"My goodness! No wonder you're pale. Mr. Roth demands a tight security here. He won't be happy to hear about this." She took a pen and wrote something down.

I took another sip of water. "It upset me more than I realized."

"I'll speak to Ben about it after I've settled you in. Now, just put it out of your mind, dearie." Her face held genuine concern.

"I'll be fine."

"As soon as we finish here, I'll show you to your room to rest from your long trip. I'm not sure how much you've been told about the position before you accepted. You will tutor Mr. Roth's ward, Ellen, soon to be six years old. She suffers from chronic asthma and has a full-time nurse."

"I wasn't told about that." I pulled myself together to pay attention to Mrs. Chambers.

"You'll meet Ellen and Nurse Clayton at dinner tonight. Tomorrow you'll begin teaching."

"Do I report to you or Mr. Roth?"

"Oh, not me dearie, you report directly to Mr. Roth."

"When will I meet him?" Did I have fantasies about the master of the mansion? Yes, but I was also realistic. It was just that, a fantasy, right?

"He's in Boston today, and expected after dinner. Oh, and before I forget," Mrs. Chambers opened a desk drawer, retrieving a key on a fob. "This unlocks the side gate from the outside at the main entrance, where you first met Ben. You don't need it to leave the grounds." She stood and motioned me to follow her.

I put the key in my bag and we went up a dimly lit back stairway.

She paused on the first floor, and she pointed to a door. "This goes to the foyer. The dining room is through there. I'm sorry I don't have time to give you the full tour today."

"That's fine," I murmured as we continued up the stairs.

"We'll do it tomorrow when I take you up to the classroom. Hasn't been used in years, so it's being cleaned. You'll find your way. Just ask any of the staff for directions if you're lost."

Up the stairs to the second floor, we turned into a long, wide hallway.

"This is the north wing and bedrooms for you, Nurse Clayton, and Ellen, plus a few guest rooms, though there haven't been guests since I've come here." She stopped at the first door. "This is your room. The other two along this hall are Ellen's and her nurse's. Beyond is the main stairway to the foyer."

When she opened the door, I gasped at the large and beautifully decorated room that would be mine, a mere employee. "This . . . is my room?"

"This is the grandest house I've ever worked at. Not a plain room in the mansion. Mr. Roth wanted you to be near Ellen." She smiled and pointed at a box on the wall. "If you need anything, use the intercom here. Just push the button and it will ring downstairs. If I'm not there, someone else will answer. The phone on the nightstand is for outside calls. Feel free to let your family know you arrived safely. It's on a party-line."

I doubted Orpha would be worried. She seemed happy to get rid of me. "Where is your room?"

"I have a suite connected to my office, in case you need me and I'm nowhere to be found."

"Thank you. Ben mentioned bicycles are available for staff. I'd like to go into town for a few essentials."

"Of course." She smiled and left.

Someone had delivered my suitcase and placed it at the foot of the four-poster bed. Aqua-colored floral wallpaper covered the walls framed by carved gold gilt panels. My fingers trailed the elaborately carved mahogany furniture and I thought back to my simple desk and single bed at Orpha's. The dressing table was more than I ever could have imagined and when I opened the enormous standing wardrobe, I chuckled. My few pieces of clothing would look silly in there. I hung my one nice dress and another suit, two blouses, a sweater, and a pair of slacks. How sad they looked.

Sheer white curtains graced the French doors leading out to a narrow terrace. I held onto the wrought-iron railing and inhaled the delightful fragrance of roses, hydrangeas, and dozens of other flowers from the garden below. Tall trees hid the ocean beyond, but I could taste the salty sea as I wrapped my arms around myself. It was heaven.

After sitting on the train and bus, my body craved some exercise. There was plenty of time to ride into Plymouth before dinner. After freshening up and changing into a pair of trousers, I found my way back down the back stairs to the courtyard. The bicycles were lined up in a row alongside the garage wall. I selected a ladies' bike with a basket and a little bell. Ben came out smoking a cigarette and waved. I waved back and took off down the drive.

Approaching the main gate, I hopped off the bike, pushing it to the side exit. Unlocked, as I had been told, and once through, headed down the highway toward the town, keeping to the side. Few cars passed me by. One with a family. A child waved at me from the back seat. An old pickup truck with workers in the truck bed. I came upon a curve in the road with tall shrubs that blinded me from oncoming traffic. Just as I turned, a sports-car came straight at me. The driver was leaning over. I veered off the road and landed in a bush flat on my behind. Not hurt, but angry at the driver, who obviously wasn't paying attention. I stood and brushed myself off.

"Miss, are you alright?" said a man's voice from behind.

It was the man from the car. He had pulled over to the side of the road and walked toward me. The wind whipped through his longish, dark, wavy hair, framing a strikingly handsome face. As he came closer, his crystal light blue eyes caught me off guard.

"I'm fine, no thanks to you." My voice was curt as I stood straight with my feet planted.

"Sorry. I didn't see you."

"I suppose not, since you weren't even looking at the road. Your head was down as I saw your car coming at me."

"Yes. Bad habit. Messing with the damn radio. Don't know why they put it below the dash. You were too far into the road."

"I beg your pardon? I was riding on the shoulder. Besides, how could you know where I was if you didn't see me?"

"When I looked up, I saw you on the road veering off."

"I was not!" I glared. "Now, if you don't mind. I need to get to town."

"I'll take you." He reached for my bike and I yanked it away from him.

"There's no room for a bicycle in that tiny excuse for a vehicle." I couldn't believe the words pouring from my mouth. It was actually a very expensive Mercedes-Benz Roadster. Before he saw my embarrassment, I hopped on the bicycle and rode away as fast as I could.

"I didn't get your name," he shouted.

I looked behind me. He was still standing with his hands on his hips, watching me.

Upset by the interaction with such an infuriating man, I swore to myself as I rode down the coast highway. Soon it turned into the main street that ran through town.

The buildings were charming white planked siding and typical coastal New England architecture. I parked the bike outside a small department store where I purchased a few personal items and a green shirtwaist dress with short, white cuffed sleeves. The basket on the bicycle just barely held my packages.

When I returned to Rothmorton, Mrs. Chambers was in her office.

"Sorry to bother you. Could I borrow an iron to press my clothes?"

"Certainly. I'll send someone up with one and a board. Oh, and dinner won't be until later, at seven o'clock, in the first-floor dining room. Mr. Roth called right after you arrived. He'll be here for dinner."

I thanked her and went straight to my room. A few minutes later, Belinda, a bubbly young maid in her late teens, delivered an iron and a board. I took my time getting ready for dinner, feeling anxious about meeting everyone, particularly Mr. Roth. Would he be like Mr. Rochester? As much as I liked the novel, I hoped Mr. Roth would be different. I had dated a few boys in college for a Friday night movie, though nothing serious. After graduating, I focused on teaching and helping Orpha on the farm. I convinced myself there wasn't time for dating, though I wondered if I was avoiding it. As much as I wanted to find love, the immaturity of the boys I met magnified my inexperience and insecurity.

I wore my new dress, adding a dab of Evening in Paris cologne, and stepped out into the hall, unsure which way to go, when a door opened. A woman with black hair pulled back in a nurse's cap, wearing a white uniform, stepped into the hall followed by a little blonde curly-haired girl in a blue dress with a Peter Pan collar and black patent Mary Jane's with white anklets. I went toward them to introduce myself.

"You're the tutor, aren't you?" the little girl said.

"Yes, I'm Dee Danes. You must be Ellen."

"I'm supposed to call you Miss Danes. Just like going to school."

Such an adorable child, all smiles with a missing front tooth. I couldn't help but smile back.

"Glad to meet you, Ellen. I'm excited to teach you," I said.

The woman eyed me with curiosity and held out her hand. "I'm Nurse Clayton, but you can call me Sylvi in private." Her tone civil.

I sensed caution and wondered why. "You can call me Dee." I shook her hand. "Shall we?" I motioned for them to lead the way, since I was not exactly sure where to find the dining room.

Following them down the curved staircase were several large portraits hung on the wall. I wondered if Mr. Roth's portrait was there, but they all looked painted a long time ago. Nothing recent.

The sight of the dining room almost made me laugh out loud. A ridiculously long table with enough high-backed chairs to seat twenty guests dominated the space, with sideboards along two walls. They draped one end of the table with a white linen tablecloth and place settings for the four of us. Sylvi and Ellen took the two seats on one side and I took the seat on the side with only one place setting. We exchanged some pleasantries, then several minutes passed in awkward silence. Just as I opened my mouth to speak, the sound of quick, firm footsteps on the marble floor caused us to turn.

Of all people, the man with the roadster entered the room and took the empty seat at the head of the table. My mouth dropped open when a rush of warmth flooded my face as I realized with whom I had spoken so brashly.

CHAPTER TWO

"My apologies, ladies," Mr. Roth said. His gaze moved around the table at each of us until he stopped with me. "Ah, you must be the new tutor for Ellen." He tilted his head with an expression not lending a hint we had met that afternoon, though without introduction.

His attire was unexpected and casual, I thought, for dinner in a mansion. He wore no jacket, a white long-sleeved dress shirt opened at the throat, no tie. There was a ruggedness to his appearance, his tanned skin, broad shoulders, and powerful hands. Certainly not what I had expected for a wealthy business executive who spent most of his days, I assumed, in an office.

"Yes, Sir, I am Dee Danes." I followed his lead by acting as if we had never seen each other before.

He made a crooked smile, extending his hand, which I took and he gave it a firm shake, then turned to the others.

At once, I realized the similarity between my run-in with Mr. Roth in his car and Jane's meeting with Mr. Rochester on his horse, with a very significant difference. It was I who spoke harshly to Mr. Roth. In the book, it was Mr. Rochester who spoke harshly to Jane.

"I assume you've all introduced yourselves. As you can see, Miss Danes, we don't stand on tradition by dressing for dinner. You must have guessed in advance by the looks of your house dress."

My eyes lowered to my dress, suddenly ashamed I'd considered it suitable, when in fact, as he so blatantly pointed out, it was nothing more than a house dress, at least in his world. Humiliated, I glanced up at him. He showed no animosity, his face calmly assessing my response. Was he retaliating for my earlier behavior? As if he had a right. He was the one who almost ran me over. Despite my irritation with him, the situation had me at a disadvantage. He was my employer and demanded respect or my new job could end before it started. Swallowing my pride, I forced a defiant smile.

He picked up a tiny bell and gave it a couple of rings and a young man entered, dressed in a white jacket, black pants, and bowtie, carrying a silver platter with bowls of soup he placed in front of us. Ellen chattered on about her day with Sylvi. When the main course was served, roast beef, rosemary potatoes, and asparagus with hollandaise, my mind wandered, thinking it seemed strange the servant wore a tie, yet Mr. Roth did not. I recognized the dishes from The Ladies' Home Journal I read every month, wishing I could taste the sumptuous foods in the pictures. In Orpha's home, it was plain dull fare. If I tried making something new or more creative, she would turn up her nose and tell me I should stop trying to be someone I wasn't.

And here I was in a fabulous mansion being served fancy foods. If it hadn't been for the sour taste in my mouth from Mr. Roth's comments, everything would have been perfect.

"Uncle Hugh, isn't Miss Danes pretty?"

He stopped eating, turned and leaned closer to me, studying my face. "I believe you are right. She is pretty, indeed."

I ignored his compliment, thinking it didn't excuse his earlier rude remark about my dress, so I looked across the table at Ellen.

"I can't wait until tomorrow for my first day of school." She grinned at me and then at her uncle.

He had finally stopped staring at me, addressing Ellen. "Good to hear, pumpkin."

"I'm excited about tomorrow, too, Ellen." I took a bite of the most tender roast beef I'd ever had and moaned. "This is delicious."

"I'll let the chef know." Mr. Roth eyed me again.

I took another bite.

"What time will you need Ellen in the classroom?" Sylvi asked.

"How about nine o'clock?" I covered my mouth with my hand. Why did I take such a huge bite?

"We'll be there," Sylvi said.

When we all finished eating, Mr. Roth rose, turning to me. "We usually retire to the library for drinks and cards or listen to the radio until it's Ellen's bedtime."

I nodded.

Ellen took her uncle's hand, and Sylvi and I followed behind.

The library gave me a warm and inviting feeling with the rich dark wood paneling, cozy overstuffed club chairs, a wing-back chair near the formidable fireplace, and plush tufted sofa where Ellen and her uncle sat deep in conversation, such as it could be with a six-year-old. Sylvi went to sit at the leather-covered card table and began a game of solitaire.

There were shelves full of books from the floor to the extremely high ceiling, and I noted many familiar classics and some foreign titles. I paused at the Louis XVI desk between two double French doors, and viewed the wall next to it covered with photos from Mr. Roth's schools, a prep academy glee club, college crew team, diplomas, and degrees in elaborate frames. There weren't any family photos, except for an elegant framed photo of Ellen on the desk. I assumed he was unmarried, no wife at dinner, nor one mentioned, and I guessed he was early thirties.

I leaned against the desk and observed Ellen talking with her hands animated in the air as she chatted while Mr. Roth studied her. His face had fallen from some thoughts. When Ellen stopped talking, he came to and caught me watching him. I feigned disinterest by picking up a magazine about yachting from the desk.

"Miss Danes, care for a game of cards?" Sylvi said.

"Sure," I took the seat opposite her. "What do you usually play?"

"Gin Rummy sound good?"

I nodded an affirmative and Sylvi dealt out seven cards for each of us. Mr. Roth's occasional stare distracted my attention. Because of our altercation that afternoon and his insult at dinner, I disliked him and worried I made a terrible mistake in taking the job.

Watching him with Ellen, so attentive to her chatter, it was obvious he cared very much for his ward, almost as if she were his own daughter. It warmed my heart, despite my determination to remain aloof.

Mr. Roth tweaked Ellen's cheek. "It's time for bed, sweetheart." He motioned to Sylvi. The two of them went to the door when Ellen stopped and turned around.

"Goodnight, Miss Danes." Her face lit up with the most charming little smile.

"Sweet dreams, Ellen." Finding myself alone with Mr. Roth, I rose from the card table, unsure what to do.

He calmly observed me for a moment. "Are you tired? It's been a long day for you."

"Not yet." I lied, not wanting him to think I was one of those frail women.

"Come, sit. I want to know more about you." He motioned to a chair opposite him.

I sat with my hands folded in my lap.

"First, I apologize once again for almost running you down today."

"I was upset and did not know who you were."

"Well, you didn't give me much of a chance, riding off so fast." He laughed, making his blue eyes crinkle and his face light up.

I bit my lip to restrain myself from making a snide remark and hopefully, showed a calm exterior.

He lounged against the cordovan leather sofa, one arm resting along the back, and the other with his hand dangling from the end of the armrest. A large gold ring with a black stone setting centered with a diamond, elegant yet understated, adorned his middle finger. "Tell me about yourself." His eyes bored into mine, as if trying to read my mind.

Unnerved, I stuttered like a schoolgirl, as if I were speaking to a boy for the first time. "W-well . . . after graduating from Teacher's College, I taught for one year in—"

"No, no, not what I know from your application. I want to learn about you, your family, your interests." His rich baritone voice softened, similar to how he spoke to Ellen.

"I have little family and lived with my second cousin on her farm."

"When did you lose your parents?" He leaned forward with his arms resting on his knees.

Taken aback by his accurate assumption and his familiarity, I relaxed. "They died in an automobile accident when I was seven." Another surprise, by divulging personal information normally kept private.

"I'm terribly sorry. My mother died when I was around that age. Siblings?"

"Sorry for your loss, too. I am an only child."

"So am I . . . interesting." He leaned back into the sofa, his eyes curious as his fingers whisked his chin. "Where did you go? Family I suspect."

"Not right away. I lived in an institution until a cousin took me in." Again, more personal information I never divulge. What was it about him that made me open up so easily?

"Good God, no! How terrible for you. What was that like?"

His sincerity was so unexpected, it touched me, making it very difficult to dislike him, but the protective walls I had developed since childhood rose around me and I shutdown.

"I'd rather not, if you don't mind." I had pushed memories from those two miserable years far deep inside me and I did not want them to surface in front of my employer.

"Of course, didn't mean to pry. I find it interesting we have that in common."

"I suppose, if you mean losing a mother."

"And neither of us have siblings."

"Right. What about your family? Your father?"

"Ah yes, dear beloved Father. He passed six years ago." He rolled his eyes.

Did I denote a tone of sarcasm? I guessed he and his father didn't get along.

"May I pour you a drink? Wine?"

"No, thank you." I fidgeted with my hanky, my nervousness returning. He made me comfortable and nervous at the same time. How was that possible?

He went to a burl wood mobile bar with a built-in radio and phonograph. There were glasses on one side, and decanters on the other. He poured himself a short glass of an amber-colored liquid. I had limited exposure to drinking since Orpha prohibited alcohol at home.

"Father left me everything, including his seat as Chairman of the Board of Rothmorton Insurance. We serve the shipping industry. Very lucrative."

"I see."

"Boston is close enough to go in regularly, for meetings and such. I do as much as possible from here. Being near Ellen is important."

"That's admirable. She's a lovely child."

"Ellen is a bright spot in my life and she's not even mine." He laughed like it was a joke and I should have known the punchline. "A very distant cousin died and named me as guardian to Ellen. I was surprised and relieved."

"Relieved? You know, I'll take a small glass of wine after all."

"How about some port? It's great after dinner."

I nodded, having no idea what port was. He poured the dark red liquid into a beautifully etched wineglass and handed it to me with a flourish.

I took a sip. "It's sweet. I like it."

"You blush easily, Miss Danes."

I touched my face, and it was warm. *Not again.*

"It's all right. I find it quite becoming on you."

"Thank you. I think."

"You questioned why I was relieved about Ellen. Loneliness, I suppose. She filled the house with her adorable laughter. She was only two. I had the nursery revived and filled with toys, and hired a nanny to care for her."

"Was she sick then, too?"

"Didn't know how serious it was until she turned four. I thought it best to have a trained nurse. It was frightening to see a child suffer so to breathe. I could hardly bear it."

"How awful." I set my empty glass on the side table. His fluid conversation surprised me and the wine changed my mood to amiable.

"Things settled down with the right care. Probably over watched her. I worry, you know. It was unfortunate her nurse married and moved away."

"Really? When was that?"

"Oh, a couple of months ago. We hired Nurse Clayton and now you. Ellen will need time to adjust. She's a good kid."

"She's lucky to have you."

He sat down again on the sofa. His expression went dark. "Ellen lucky? I suppose she is, in a way. Like you, an orphan."

I said nothing, thinking what a stupid thing I said. How was being an orphan lucky? It certainly hadn't been for me. Even with all his money, she was still without parents and an only child like him and me. The mood had turned depressing. I looked around the room.

"You look tired now."

I gave him a wan smile. "I am tired. But what about your expectations?"

"What?" He looked confused.

"Regarding my tutoring Ellen?"

"Right. I will leave it for you. You have the expertise and know what Ellen needs to learn."

"I appreciate your confidence. I was wondering . . . with Boston so close by, why did you advertise so far away?"

"I sent out advertisements all over the country, Miss Danes. I was looking for a different point of view than what we would find nearby. Your letters of recommendations and your essay on why you want to be a tutor impressed me. I'm confident you were the right choice."

There was something in his expression that caused me to think he was not being truthful. I couldn't put my finger on it, but it was there, nevertheless. "Thank you. Hope I don't let you down." That was if I stayed.

We rose and bid each other a good night. He poured another drink as I left the library. I wondered how many he would have, though it shouldn't have concerned me.

In my room, I pondered on my employer. I didn't like him. He was insulting despite his apology and pleasantness in the library. His comment on my dress brought back humiliations I had endured as a child. Losing both my parents devastated me and not one adult offered me comfort. The other children at the orphanage weren't any better off than me. They somehow made me feel inferior. I swore not to let that happen ever again, but I had failed repeatedly. My feelings of inferiority get the better of me, regardless.

And then there was the sadness I saw in Mr. Roth's eyes, and my concern over his truthfulness or lack thereof. What could it be? Maybe fear of being found out. About what? What secrets would someone like him have?

My impulsive decision to uproot myself and move halfway across the country taking this job was looking like Orpha might have been right. Not only that, but the memory of the dead cat was another reason for concern. I may have made the worse mistake of my life.

CHAPTER THREE

I hurried down the main staircase, having overslept and afraid I missed breakfast. Belinda was busy dusting the foyer furniture as I passed her, heading to the dining room. It was empty.

"Breakfast is in the downstairs staff dining area," she said.

"That's right, I forgot. Thank you."

When I reached the lower level, Mrs. Chambers sat alone in the dining area.

"There you are, Miss Danes." Mrs. Chambers gave me a cheerful smile, folding the morning paper. "I wondered what happened."

"I couldn't recall what time breakfast was served. Would it be an inconvenience for just an egg and toast, and lots of coffee?"

"Did I forget to tell you we served breakfast down here for staff daily between six-thirty and eight o'clock AM? I'm very sorry. There was a lot going on yesterday. It's just now eight, so there is still plenty of food for you. It's on the sideboard."

"Oh good. Where are Ellen and Nurse Clayton?"

"They left a while ago. Ellen usually plays in the nursery after breakfast. Nurse Clayton will bring Ellen to the classroom, I suspect."

"Yes, at nine."

The display of food was generous. Chafing dishes of scrambled eggs, bacon, sausage, shredded fried potatoes, a fruit platter, juice, and all sorts of pastries and toast. It made me hungry, and I filled a plate, taking a seat across from Mrs. Chambers.

"What about Mr. Roth?" I asked.

"He's an early bird and takes breakfast alone. When he works from here, he spends the day in the library. I'll wait for you to finish and then take you up to the third-floor classroom."

I ate quickly and drank the coffee in gulps, needing it to become fully awake.

"Okay, I'm ready."

"I thought I'd finish showing you the formal rooms. Mr. Roth has entertained little in the five years I've been here. There hasn't been so much as a dinner party, except for Ellen's birthday celebrations. Strange, if you ask me. I won't complain, a lot less work than trying to keep a household like this one clean and guest ready."

We entered the parlor. Another spacious room with chandeliers and gold gilt everywhere imaginable, casting sparkles of light throughout. The drapes and upholstery coordinated in hues of vivid dark pink, red, gold stripes, and florals, with oriental carpets over the same marble flooring as in the foyer.

"Simply stunning," I said.

"We use the parlor for visiting guests on the rare occasion."

I followed her to the foyer and through another door.

"This is the music room."

The room was empty, except for a concert grand piano at the farthest end. Light reflected from the mirrored walls. The four chandeliers were even more extravagant than in the other rooms.

"Is this room used as a ballroom?" I asked.

"It's designed for dancing and why a parquet wood floor instead of the marble. See the raised dais for an orchestra?"

"Must have been grand to attend a ball here."

"I imagine so. Mr. Roth uses this room for Ellen's party and usually hires a string quartet to play. For a child, it's a very formal event."

"How odd." I whispered to myself. "I've never been to a formal birthday party . . . *for anyone*."

Mrs. Chambers was way ahead of me. I had to step quickly to catch up. As we went up the curved stairway in the foyer, I asked, "I don't see a portrait of Mr. Roth."

"He doesn't have one."

I wondered why.

On to the third floor, north wing, a walkway ran around the staircase to the hallway on the west side. She stopped at the first door on the left and unlocked it, handing me the key, and I put it on the key fob.

"You won't need to lock it each day. Ellen is the only student."

"My goodness. It's large enough for ten children."

There were only two children's sized desks facing one wall where a chalk board stood on a wooden stand.

"When the estate was first built, I imagined they expected to have lots of children. They only had one son, Mr. Roth's father. I heard rumors there were several miscarriages and a little girl who didn't live past two," Mrs. Chambers said.

"How sad. Everything looks brand new?"

"Yes, amazing, isn't it?"

"They must be from the same period they built the house, around 1885?"

"I believe so."

"So, Mr. Roth sat in here as a child, and maybe his father, too?"

"I think so. I'll leave you to prepare for Ellen's lessons. Let me know if you need anything. You can order books by phoning the bookstore in Plymouth. The number is on your desk. I'll see you at lunch." She left, leaving the door open.

I stood at the windows facing the west overlooking the front circular driveway and fountain. The lack of morning sun made the room chillier. The wall thermometer confirmed at 68 degrees. A shiver ran up my arms, partly from nervousness, though my skirted suit was warm enough.

Orpha was to ship my winter clothes to me. I only hoped my attire would meet Mr. Roth's standards. If I stayed that long. I scanned the bookshelves for teaching material and found them to be outdated, except for the McGuffey Readers first published in the nineteenth century and still widely used. The popular Dick and Jane Readers would need to be ordered. Since those books focused on a typical two-parent family structure, I wasn't sure if it would be appropriate for Ellen. I would order them anyway, just in case.

A quick look at my wristwatch, and it was a little before nine o'clock. I sat at the teacher's desk next to the window across from the student's desks. In the desk drawers were a stenographer's notebook, fountain pens, and pencils. I jotted down some ideas on lessons. A noise in the doorway made me look up. Ellen ran in, followed by Sylvi.

"Miss Danes!" Ellen said as a glorious smile lit up her charming face framed with a bounty of ringlets. She reminded me of Shirley Temple. She peered over the top of my desk. "I'm happy to see you. What'll we do today?"

"Go sit down at one of those desks and then I'll tell you." I glanced at Nurse Clayton. "If we need you, how may I find you?"

She gave a startled look, as if she expected to stay during the lessons. "Use the intercom to Mrs. Chambers' office. She or someone else down there will intercom me in my room. Unless I decide to take a walk, I'll let Mrs. Chambers know where I am."

"Thank you. I expect we will break for lunch at eleven-thirty downstairs."

"I'll be there. When will Ellen's lessons end?"

"At three o'clock."

"May I speak to you privately before I leave?"

"Of course. Ellen, start reading this book until I return." I placed the first edition of Winnie the Pooh in front of her.

"Oh, I love bears," Ellen said.

We went into the hallway out of earshot of Ellen.

"Has anyone explained to you Ellen's health issues?"

"She has asthma, though I know little about it other than breathing issues."

"Ellen's condition has been a cause for alarm frequently and why she needs a nurse. She's also been hospitalized for serious symptoms."

"I didn't know. Do you think you should sit in on Ellen's studies? I figured you needed some time to yourself?"

"No one said anything to me. But I could use the time."

"What if something happens and we need you?"

"Certain situations can cause an episode, such as sudden temperature changes, catching cold, or extreme emotions. As long as you keep your time with her somewhat stable, it should be fine. I won't be far away though if she wheezes or complains she can't breathe. Just find me right away. We have a nebulizer in her room for emergencies. It helps clear her passageways."

"I understand, and thanks for explaining all this to me. Would you like to get together after Ellen goes to bed? We could get to know each other."

"I'd like that. I'll see the two of you at lunch." She turned and went down the hall.

Worried something might happen while alone with Ellen plagued me. I hoped it was not a mistake letting the nurse leave. It would have been uncomfortable with her watching me on my first day.

Since there didn't appear to be a clear set of rules or time frames for tutoring, it was up to me. Nine to three for a six-year-old, getting personal instruction seemed fully adequate. Assumed lunch would be about an hour, I was comfortable with the plan.

Ellen had taken a seat at the smaller of the two student desks. To be at her level, I squeezed into the other desk, wondering which one Mr. Roth would have used.

"Now Ellen, have you learned your alphabet?"

She nodded.

"And can you write your full name?"

"Uh huh, do you want me to show you?"

"In a minute. Have you done any reading?"

"Some I can read without help. Some are too hard."

After several more questions, I determined she was a tad behind. Her positive interest in learning was encouraging. Nothing worse than trying to teach someone who didn't want to be there. I started her out doing some penmanship exercises on lined paper. When she picked up the pencil with her left hand, I smiled. I was left-handed, too.

"Do you use your left hand for everything?" I asked.

"I don't know. Why?"

"Just curious. Who taught you how to write and learn your alphabet?"

"My nurse. Not Nurse Clayton, the one before her. She was nice, got married and moved away."

"Miss Clayton hasn't worked here for very long?"

"Uh-uh, a little while."

"Do you understand why you have a nurse?"

"Uh-huh, sometimes I can't breathe good. Uncle Hugh doesn't like it."

Ellen had a handle on her life. Probably because it was all she'd known since she was so young.

"Do you remember when you came to live here?"

"I've always lived here."

Not remembering she lived elsewhere was a lucky thing for Ellen. I envied her not living in an institution, though fewer existed these days. She was young enough not to remember. I wished I couldn't. My mind wandered to my childhood, bullied by unkind children no better off than myself. I didn't understand such behavior. It impressed upon me to the degree that I fell into fantasies. My imagination protected me, I supposed.

"All right, Ellen, I'd like to hear you read for me." I handed her the first-grade reader from the bookshelf and Ellen read out loud in a halting manner.

By lunchtime, we had moved onto working with numbers and she did well.

"Ready for a break?"

"Yes, Miss Danes. I like being with you." Her face lit up again, and she jumped up from the desk, her blond curls dancing. "Let's go, I'm hungry."

As promised, Sylvi met us in the staff dining area. Mrs. Chambers sat at the head of the table, while one of the kitchen staff placed cold meats and cheeses for sandwiches on the sideboard. It was help yourself as was breakfast.

"Do you want me to make a sandwich for you?" I asked Ellen, who took the seat to Mrs. Chambers's left.

"I'll do it." Sylvi interjected and prepared two plates.

I stepped aside, since I didn't know what Ellen liked anyway, and prepared myself a roast beef sandwich, spooned a colorful fruit salad into a bowl, and took a seat at the table on Mrs. Chambers's right.

"How did it go?" Sylvi asked as she placed a plate with a half sandwich and fruit in front of Ellen.

"Thank you, Nurse Clayton. Fine. It's fun reading and writing," Ellen said.

"She's bright and a quick learner," I said.

Sylvi and Mrs. Chambers nodded in agreement while eating.

The rest of the staff made their way in and Mrs. Chambers introduced to me to two house maids, middle-aged Clara and Belinda, who I had already met. Ben strolled in and promptly took the empty chair next to me with a great big smile on his face. I noticed he gave a wink to Belinda, making me wonder if there was something between them. I thought her much too young for him.

There was Charlie, a Negro in his sixties, and his crew of two young men from Puerto Rico, who sat together at the end of the table. Robert, the chef who looked around the same age as the housekeeper, placed a large plate of pastries in the middle of the table before seating himself at the other end opposite Mrs. Chambers. The assistant chef took the last seat.

Voices clamored over each other while I struggled in vain to remember the names to the faces, wishing we all had name tags. They were a friendly and open group. I listened while they shared where they came from and when. Most hadn't been at Rothmorton for longer than five years. I calculated many things occurred around five years ago: Mr. Roth's father passed away, Ellen came, Mrs. Chambers started working there and one housemaid. Maybe when his father died, he wanted his stamp on things. Except for Charlie, who had been there longer than anyone.

Belinda bubbled with high energy and animated speech. "Did you know Miss Danes Rothmorton Hall is supposed to be haunted?" She giggled.

"Is it?" I raised my eyebrows in disbelief.

"Nonsense," Mrs. Chambers said. "The house is shifting, is all. It's nothing."

"Not what I heard," Ben said. "I've seen wisps in the night." He cast a sly glance at me.

"You have not!" Ellen said, laughing. "You can't scare me."

"I'm not trying to scare you, little one," Ben said.

"Well, I don't believe in ghosts," I said.

"Ditto," said Sylvi.

Robert piped in. "Well, I for one believe in 'em. Pretty sure something passed by the round window on the second floor. It was the other morning, before the sun came up."

"I know it wasn't me or Ellen," said Sylvi. "You must have imagined it."

"Enough talk about things going bump in the night. I've never seen a ghost and I don't believe any of you have either," Mrs. Chambers said.

Everyone laughed in good fun.

Ellen turned to Mrs. Chambers. "Have you seen my cat?"

"You don't have a cat, dearie," Mrs. Chambers said.

"Yes, I do. She's gray with a white face. I feed her outside after breakfast. She didn't come this morning."

I shot a worried look at Mrs. Chambers, and she shrugged her shoulders with indifference, and then I glanced at Ben. He wasn't even listening. "Sorry, Ellen," I said. "Maybe she returned to where she came from?"

"I miss her." Ellen's face fell and my heart lurched for her.

"Don't worry," Sylvi patted Ellen's hand, "maybe she will turn up. Just remember not to get too close. You know cats aren't good for your asthma."

"I know." The corners of Ellen's mouth turned down.

The bloody image of Ellen's cat on the tree came to mind, and I shuddered. It made little sense to me why anyone want to hurt Ellen by killing an animal she loved. I wondered if I should tell Sylvi about it, but what could she do? Mrs. Chambers assured me Mr. Roth would be told.

Lunch was over and Ellen and I returned to the classroom to finish out the day with some geography about Massachusetts. With the lessons done,

I ordered the new readers and some other books by calling the bookstore in Plymouth. They would deliver the books to the estate.

***

Around five o'clock, I was passing through the first floor toward the garden when the library door swung open, nearly hitting me in the face.

"Oh, I didn't see you there. Are you alright?" Mr. Roth reached a hand for me, but I withdrew.

"I'm okay, just startled. You're in an awful hurry." I stepped aside.

"Sorry, yes, and behind. I've got dinner out, so I won't see you till tomorrow. Please tell Ellen. I'm sorry I didn't have a chance to tell her."

"Of course." And he was off up the stairs, taking two at a time. Business meeting, I supposed, but why the urgency?

***

After dinner, Sylvi, Ellen and I went to the library to listen to the evening radio news program and some music. When it was Ellen's bedtime, I flipped through a magazine until Sylvi returned for our chat. About twenty minutes later, she peeked in the door.

"You still up for our chat?"

"Sure, come on in. Would you like a drink? Some port?" I said, getting up to pour myself a small glass from the bar acting as if I'd done it a million times before.

"Sure, sounds good."

We clinked our glasses together. An awkward moment passed. I didn't know the next thing to say.

"So, why a tutor? Didn't you teach in the school system?"

I took a seat in one of the overstuffed club chairs and crossed my legs, leaning back. Sylvi took the other chair.

"I taught a year in the local elementary school for experience. I had issue with the discipline allowed in the schools. Too harsh."

"Corporal punishment? We all had it."

"Doesn't make it right or beneficial. But I'd spent my life in rural Illinois. It was time for a change."

"Makes sense, though it's still rural here."

"Somewhat, but Boston is a heck of a lot closer than any large town where I lived."

"I wonder why Mr. Roth hired a teacher from another state and not local? Though I'm sure you are qualified."

I shrugged my shoulders, not wanting to repeat my conversation with Mr. Roth. "I'm grateful to be here." A white lie. Because I had been so excited when I received the job offer. "I pleaded with the college placement office to find something far away. When the advertisement arrived, I thought it was a sign." Though I was thinking about quitting, I wouldn't tell Sylvi about my concerns before I decided.

"Good for you. I'm all for going after what you want." She raised her glass up in the air to me.

"What about you? You don't have the New England sound in your voice."

"No. I've lived around, and served as a nurse during the war, then afterwards in New York City. I needed a change from the hospital scene and thought taking care of one patient would be a pleasant change, and it is. Ellen is a darling."

"She is." I observed Sylvi while she talked, thinking her reasons were as vague as mine. What does it take for someone to uproot themselves to work at a secluded estate? I could only answer the question for myself. Maybe in time, Sylvi would too.

We continued talking in the same friendly yet vague generalities of our lives without getting too personal. I grew tired, and we both agreed to call it a night and headed up the stairs together to our respective rooms.

My first night, I had been so exhausted I slept like a rock. But, the second night, the creaks and groans the house made disturbed me and I recalled the conversation during lunch about the house being haunted. I shivered in my bed, sure I heard footsteps in the hall. The clock said one o'clock. Good grief, who was running down the hall at this time of night? I pulled on my robe and opened the door a couple of inches, peeking out. The dimly lit hall was quiet. No one was there. I tiptoed down to the end of the hall to the large, round-paned window, where Robert said he had seen a ghost. I looked behind me, just in case, then surveyed the garage courtyard below. In the moonlight, a woman moved away from the house, stopping at the door to the second-floor residences. Someone opened the door, and she went inside. Who was at the door?

Could have been the young maid that lives on the lower level. Or Sylvi. Who was she visiting in the middle of the night? Ben or the assistant chef? Belinda was awfully young to be associating with either of those men. It wouldn't surprise me if it were Ben. He flirted with all the women.

Sylvi lived on my floor. Was it her footsteps I heard? And why would she be running? Definitely not a ghost. I may have imagined the sound of footsteps, but not the woman in the courtyard.

I headed back to my room, when I saw Mr. Roth on the main stairway landing, looking at me. He wore a dinner suit and tie, though loosened, and the top button undone.

"Miss Danes, why are you up so late?" he said in a hushed voice.

"I thought I heard someone running down the hall and I came out to see."

"Who?" He took a few steps toward me.

Realizing my attire, I pulled my robe around me. "I don't know. I might have imagined it. There were jokes at lunch today about ghosts." I laughed too loud and covered my mouth.

He stopped halfway. "No ghosts here. Trust me. I didn't see anyone when I came in." He looked down. "Your feet are bare. Don't you own any slippers?"

I glanced at my feet. "Of course, I own slippers," I snapped back. "Didn't think I needed them on the carpeted hallway."

He chuckled, holding up his hands. "No need to be defensive. Don't want you to catch a cold your first day on the job. Get some rest and I'll see you tomorrow."

Without replying, I entered my room wanting to slam the door shut, but stamped my foot instead. What an insufferable man. Does he enjoy insulting me? Still wide awake, I kept the reading light on and wrote in my journal.

CHAPTER FOUR

It didn't take long for me to settle into a daily routine. Breakfast with staff, and after, Mrs. Chambers and I would linger to talk. Daily lunch with the staff and lessons with Ellen in the morning and afternoon filled the days. I was alone until dinner. Mr. Roth attended nearly every evening, and we were courteous with each other. After dinner in the library, we listened to the radio while I played cards and board games with Ellen and Sylvi. It was very family-like, or so I imagined.

Having always thought of myself as a loner, it surprised me how much I enjoyed the company. Despite my negative feelings for Mr. Roth, he was an interesting man, and he obviously loved Ellen. The staff were like an extended family. My family experiences were extremely limited. I embraced the activities, allowing myself to take part in the social interactions, while seeking my alone time.

It was one of those days. Once Ellen's lessons were over, I longed to be alone. I grabbed my notebook and pen and strolled through the rich green garden, in search of a shady spot to sit and write.

A man was busy digging a hole in one of the flower beds. He rose to wipe his brow with a kerchief and turned around. "Good afternoon," Mr. Roth said.

Startled, I stumbled, catching myself when I noticed he wore blue chambray work clothes with his sleeves rolled up to his biceps, revealing long lean muscles glistening with sweat from his labor. Failing to hide my surprise, I managed a greeting, my eyes staring at his muscular body.

"Shocked? I can tell," he said.

I pursed my lips. "Didn't expect to find you digging holes."

"Working outside releases the tension from my desk job, so to speak." He tipped back his wide-brimmed sun hat, assessing my notebook, gesturing at it. "Writing?"

"Maybe."

Charlie came up to Mr. Roth.

"You can finish this up for me." Mr. Roth handed him the shovel. "Miss Danes, this is our grounds keeper, Charlie. He keeps things looking sharp and has been since my father was a boy."

"We have lunch together with the other staff. Hello, Charlie." I turned to him with a smile.

"That's right," Mr. Roth said.

Charlie grinned. "Good day, Miss. Been meanin' to ask if you'd like fresh flowers in your room? I'd have a bouquet ready each mornin'."

"How thoughtful of you. Thank you."

Charlie proceeded to work on the hole Mr. Roth had started.

"Charlie is so accommodating," I said.

"He is. I've known him my whole life."

Mr. Roth walked alongside me as I moved toward the bench under a large shady tree on the opposite side of the garden facing the mansion. Pretending he wasn't there, I took my notebook from my bag and jotted a line or two.

"You don't draw?"

"Not a squiggly line, I'm afraid. I prefer to write."

"What do you write?"

"Poetry mostly." I kept my eyes on the page.

"I enjoy a good poem now and then. Let me read some."

"I'd rather not. It's personal, just for me."

He reached over and snatched my notebook from my lap.

"Really, Sir, please." Horrified, I reached for the notebook.

He backed away while flipping through the pages. I tried to take the notebook from him but he held it up high so I couldn't reach it.

"This is childish. Are we in kindergarten?"

He turned his back to me and read it out loud.

Of love, what is it?
A vain attempt at acceptance,
A risk of rejection.
Or one of denial or manipulation.
Oh, to feel the burn of passion,
Of one's fiery kiss.

I reached for it again. Realizing it was useless, I plopped down on the bench. For the millionth time since my arrival, my face burned with humiliation. Mr. Roth didn't appear to have noticed, for he continued to read the rest of the poem to himself.

"Miss Danes, this is beautiful. I am touched by the words and emotion. Is this from personal experience?"

"Not really."

"I don't believe you. It's someone back home, isn't it?"

"It isn't. I just read a lot of poetry.

"From college?"

"Well, okay, yes, someone from college. In the past, just stuff. Please give it back to me." There wasn't anyone, but I lied.

"Are you sure it's the past and you aren't pining for him? I might be a little jealous. Are you still in touch? Do you write him?"

"Really. Please stop. I don't like being made fun of." I became angry by this time. How could he be jealous? He was joking, and I didn't think it was funny. I tried to walk past him.

He put up his hand and stopped me. "I apologize for teasing you. It's really very good. I'm sorry about all the probing questions. Just curious if there is someone in your heart. Here is your notebook."

I put my hand on it. His hand lingered before releasing, and I shoved it back into my bag.

"Apology accepted. This is the second time I've accepted an apology from you. I hope this doesn't become a habit." With a snort, I walked away toward the ocean path, sensing his eyes on me. When I turned, he was gone. His actions infuriated me. Why did he ask if there was someone in my heart? Impossible. Thoughts of quitting swirled in my mind. Going back to Orpha made me cringe. I didn't know how much more of Mr. Roth I could take.

Giving up on doing any writing, I kept going down the path till I reach the railed walkway overlooking the cliffs by the sea. I embraced the calming effect of the surf, salt air, and the sounds of seagulls cawing. Closing my eyes while holding onto the rail, I breathed in, feeling the cool wind against my face. I momentarily forgot my angst. Despite the occasional strange interactions with Mr. Roth, my time so far at Rothmorton brought me a peace I had not known before.

When I turned to leave, I noticed something sticking up in the dirt. It looked like a tiny hand. "What on earth?" I kneeled down, dusting the dirt away and discovered it was a doll, with its head broken off and lying next to the little naked body. When I picked up the body, my stomach turned at the sight. There were pierce marks, as if someone had taken an icepick to it.

Ellen wasn't allowed out there unattended. I recognized it as one I'd seen in Ellen's playroom. It couldn't have been Ellen? I shuddered at the thought. A child would have to be very disturbed to do that to her own doll. I wrapped the head with my handkerchief and placed it and the body in my bag. I entered the garden and was about to pass Charlie, still working in the flower bed. He stopped working when he saw me and I stopped.

"Miss, don't you be frettin' over Mr. Hugh's teasin'."

"You heard him?"

"He only acts that way when he likes a gal." He wiped his brow with the back of his hand.

"I'm not a gal. I'm his employee. Why would he tease me so?"

"Like I say, he likes ya." He grinned, a smile glinting a gold tooth.

Mr. Roth's behavior was highly questionable as my employer. He may have thought he was being flirtatious, or even just interested, but it didn't make me feel any differently.

Conflicted at being both insulted and flattered, I needed to set it aside. I wasn't sure whether to tell Mr. Roth or Mrs. Chambers about the doll. I might have been making more of it than necessary, so I stored it in my room until I decided what to do.

***

After dinner, we were astonished when entering the library to find the furniture rearranged to face a brand new black boxed television where the radio used to sit, on the wall opposite the French doors.

Ellen ran straight for it, jumping up and down. "Oh goody, turn it on Uncle Hugh," Ellen said.

"Calm down. Take a seat on the sofa. I need to figure this out."

We were all excited. Even Sylvi let go her usual cool demeanor with a bright smile while we sat with Ellen, anxious for Mr. Roth to get it working. I had only seen a few television shows back in Illinois at the college. Orpha, of course, didn't buy one, saying it was a waste of money.

"Why hadn't you bought a television before?" Sylvi asked. "They've been around for ages."

My thoughts exactly and I was glad she mustered the courage to ask.

"Too focused on my work to even think of it. Thought they were just for families," he said.

"Why now?" I ventured.

"Look around, Miss Danes. Doesn't this feel like a family environment?" Mr. Roth bent his head down and became immersed in fiddling with the television and antennae.

Sylvi cast a questioning eye. I had noticed for some time the warm family feeling at our gatherings. Mr. Roth's revelation surprised me the most.

He raised his head from the antennae. "How's the picture now?"

"Just hold it there, Uncle Hugh," Ellen said. "When you move, it goes all squiggly lines and fuzzy." Ellen fidgeted in her seat, eager for the show to appear on the screen.

"Hilarious, Ellen. I want to watch too," he said.

Sylvi and I smothered a few giggles.

After more attempts at moving the antennae and dials, the picture cleared up and *The Lone Ranger Show* had just begun.

We all applauded and cheered and Mr. Roth made a flamboyant bow, then plopped in the club chair next to the sofa near me and gave me a wink. I pretended not to notice and hoped Sylvi didn't, when a rush of unwanted warmth flooded my face, recalling Charlie's comments about how Mr. Roth liked me. As infuriating as he could be, he was also very charming. I turned to Ellen. She seemed so normal and happy and I thought of the doll. She couldn't possibly have damaged her doll in that way. If not Ellen, then who?

Her little eyes glued to the images on the small screen, along with everyone else, so I joined in, forgetting about the doll and emersed myself in the family scene.

We all watched one more show and then Mr. Roth said it was enough.

"Please, just one more?" She gave him her sweetest smile and tugged on his sleeve.

"One hour only, pumpkin. New rule. Now off to bed," he said. He patted her head and kissed her cheek.

"O---kay." Ellen slid off the sofa in slow motion, as if her uncle would change his mind, and gave him one last look.

He waved her off with a gentle smile. Sylvi took Ellen's hand, and they left me alone as usual with Mr. Roth until Sylvi returned for our evening chats. I went to the bookshelves, browsing for another novel. He poured himself a drink.

"Something for you, Miss Danes?"

"A small port would be nice."

When he handed me the glass, our fingers touched for a second. A tingle ran up my arm, and my stomach tightened from a sudden nervousness.

"Mind if I smoke?" he asked.

I shook my head, and he cracked open the French Door to light a cigarette while I sipped my port and pretended to look at the books. The electricity between us was undeniable, and I hated how it made me feel—vulnerable.

"Are you still upset about this afternoon?" he said.

"Not really. It was silly of both of us."

"I agree. You are an easy mark for teasing." He shut the door and snuffed out the cigarette.

"I suppose so. Boys teased me a lot when I was younger." And I hated it every bit as much as I hated how Mr. Roth teased me. I wanted to be angry with him, but Sylvi would return soon.

"Did they?" He stepped toward me.

I grabbed a book from the shelf and hastened to a chair just as Sylvi entered. She stopped short, giving us a strange look.

He finished his drink in one gulp and set the glass down a bit too loudly. "I'll call it a night. You ladies enjoy the rest of your evening."

I bid him goodnight and opened the book I would never read, titled *Julius Caesar*. I sighed.

"What was that about?" Sylvi poured some wine.

I shrugged my shoulders, feigning ignorance, hoping she would drop it.

She took the other club chair and crossed her legs. "The tension was so thick I could cut it with a knife. Something going on between you two?"

"Hardly."

"Well, something happened."

"Nothing really. We had a kind of, oh never mind . . . it was childish."

"Come on, you can tell me."

"This afternoon, I was writing in the garden and he . . . oh, never mind. It was just silliness and embarrassing."

"If you don't want to tell me, fine. I think he likes you and not as an employee, if you get my drift."

"That would be inappropriate. He's our employer."

"What matters is how you feel about it. Don't you think?"

"I don't know. Can we talk about something else? Wasn't it fun to watch the television shows?"

Sylvi accepted my change of subject and we chatted about the shows until we were tired and went upstairs to our rooms.

I went to the terrace and watched the moon. Couldn't stop thinking about Mr. Roth. He was my employer, and I was Ellen's tutor. I needed a clear head and my mind on what was important. Even though I had fantasized about taking this job and fall in love with the master of the mansion, it couldn't happen now. I hadn't forgiven him his rudeness on my first day, and today was just compounded by everything. It only made matters worse for me. Should I go home to Orpha and admit defeat, or stay?

Even though I enjoyed Sylvi's company and hoped we could become friends, there was something mysterious about her as well. She came across so reserved. I wouldn't believe she was the woman sneaking across the courtyard. Not an unattractive woman, Sylvi had pleasant features. It was the way she wore her hair, so severe. It made her appear unapproachable. Knowing Ben, he probably would find it a challenge and then again, maybe it wasn't her or Ben.

***

Another Saturday came around and Sylvi and I switched our days off. It was my day to cover for her. When I went to Ellen's room, Sylvi was there.

"Nurse Clayton, I didn't expect to find you here. Figured you'd be sleeping in. Nice to see you out of uniform."

She glanced in the mirror at her yellow sweater and gray tweed skirt while brushing Ellen's hair. "Couldn't sleep."

"Good morning, Miss Danes," Ellen said with a wide, cheerful smile.

"Your hair looks lovely. Nice job taming those curls into soft waves, Nurse Clayton."

"Thanks. She's all yours." Sylvi set the brush on the dresser and grabbed her purse.

"How about a movie this afternoon, Ellen?" I tweaked her nose, and she giggled.

"Oh goody! Yes, yes." Ellen hugged me and I ran my fingers through her hair.

"I don't have any special plans today. Mind if I tag along?" Sylvi asked.

"Of course, what fun. Don't you think so, Ellen?"

Ellen nodded her head, jumping up and down. "Yes, yes!"

The intercom buzzed, and Sylvi answered. "Hello?"

"This is Mrs. Chambers. Is Dee there with you?"

"I am," I said.

"We're about to leave for breakfast," Sylvi said.

"Good, Mr. Roth requests you have breakfast with him in the first floor Breakfast Room," Mrs. Chambers said.

"We'll be right down." Sylvi switched off the intercom. "A first for me."

She and I exchanged surprised looks, and the three of us headed downstairs. The Breakfast Room was on the east side of the mansion. A bright, cheery room with pale green and white striped wallpaper, tall windows to let in the morning sunlight, with white wainscoting and crown molding around the ceiling. A room least like the rest of the main floor without the elaborate gold gilt and crystal chandeliers making it homey and friendly. I noticed there wasn't a buffet setup.

Mr. Roth was sitting at the head of the table reading his newspaper, wearing a knit shirt with a wide collar, his hair combed back, revealing his prominent forehead. When I passed by him, I caught a whiff of his aftershave, a scent of spice and musk, and absently let out a slight hum.

"Did you say something, Miss Danes?"

"Er, no. This is a delightful change." I took a seat at the table.

"I'm taking the day off and we haven't used this room much." He folded the newspaper and placed it on the table.

Ellen gave her uncle a big hug. "Hi, Uncle Hugh. Gee, you smell good."

He grinned and kissed her cheek. "What do you and Miss Danes have planned for today?" he asked Ellen.

"We're going to the movies."

"All of you?" he looked at me.

"Yes, Nurse Clayton will join us," I said.

A server entered and poured cups of coffee for the three adults. Glasses of orange juice were already at our place settings.

"Sounds like a nice outing. I'd like to go?" He said to me.

Surprised, I nearly choked on my coffee. "Really?"

He turned to Ellen. "What's the movie?"

"Lots of cartoons, I hope." She grinned.

"They are still showing *Lili*, a musical, with Leslie Caron." I replied. "It's a family film, so I'm sure there will be plenty of cartoons before the movie starts."

"Oh, goody." Ellen took a piece of toast and spread it with butter.

"I love musicals. Sounds good to me," Sylvi said.

"Great." He looked thoroughly pleased with himself, glowing with a contagious smile affecting all of us.

The day had taken an unexpected turn.

After breakfast, Ellen and I spent the morning reading and taking a bicycle ride around the grounds. Because the matinee was early, Mr. Roth told the chef we would take a late lunch in town.

***

When we girls went downstairs, Mr. Roth was waiting out front with the Bentley's doors opened.

"Where's Ben?" I asked.

"No need, I can drive. Hop in."

"I want to sit up front with you, Uncle Hugh?" Ellen tugged on his shirt.

"Sure thing, sweetheart."

With Ellen up front and Sylvi and me in the back, Mr. Roth drove into town. It was a bright sunny day, and Main Street was busy with shoppers. It was the first non-work-related activity since I had arrived at Rothmorton. Mr. Roth parked on the street near the theater, and bought tickets while we waited. He chose the row about midway down the aisle. Sylvi slipped in ahead of me, pulling Ellen behind her.

I gave Sylvi a strange look, which she ignored. "Ellen, don't you want to sit here next to your uncle?"

"Can I sit between you and Nurse Clayton? You're my best friends," Ellen said.

"Of course you can," Mr. Roth interjected. "Sit down, Miss Danes, I won't bite." He chuckled.

Reluctantly, I took the seat, feeling uncomfortable.

"You ladies just sit tight while I go get us some popcorn. I'll be right back," Mr. Roth said.

Sylvi spoke over Ellen. "I haven't been to a movie in ages. How 'bout you?"

"Me neither. Hadn't thought of it until today. It's easy to stay around Rothmorton and forget about the outside world."

"Well, whatever happened last night must have smoothed over. It's great your uncle came with us. Isn't it?" Sylvi nudged Ellen.

"I'm glad. What happened last night?" Ellen asked.

"Nothing, dear," Sylvi said.

"I think the cartoons are about to start," I said.

Mr. Roth returned to his seat with a cardboard holder containing four bags of popcorn and passed them down. When he handed a bag to me, I fumbled and popcorn spilled out into my lap.

"Darn," I said.

"Sorry, let me help you." He brushed the popcorn off my lap.

"I've got it, thanks." His touch on my thighs was almost too much to bear. I was nervous enough. I had to remind myself how much he infuriated me.

"Here, have mine. It's still full," he said.

"No. I'll take the other one."

He shrugged and settled back into his seat as the lights dimmed and the cartoons began. Ellen leaned forward with her arms resting on the seat in front of her. Thankfully, the theater wasn't very full, and no one sat in that row.

Mr. Roth's elbow rested on the armrest between us and I tried hard to keep my arm from touching his. Instead, he seemed to lean into me. I could feel his eyes on me instead of the screen and I dared not turn to look.

"You're so tense, Miss Danes," he whispered in my ear. "Relax and enjoy the movie."

"I am." I gave him the smallest smile possible.

The film was entertaining, and my mood improved. He had stopped watching me to watch the movie, and I enjoyed the warmth of his arm close to mine. The initial electricity between us had morphed into a gentle vibration.

After the movie, we walked down to the deli for sandwiches and Coca-Cola. When we returned to Rothmorton, Mr. Roth ordered up ice cream sundaes from the kitchen and we sat on the veranda overlooking the garden.

"Did you enjoy today?" Mr. Roth asked Ellen.

"Sure did. When can we go again? It was fun with all of us." She took a huge spoonful of the ice cream into her mouth and her eyes grew big and swallowed, then she choked. "Ooh, cold, cold!"

"Be more careful, Ellen," chided Nurse Clayton.

I reached over with a napkin to catch dribbles of ice cream running down Ellen's chin.

"There you go. That happens to me all the time when I eat it too fast. Better now?"

"Thank you, Miss Danes," Ellen squeaked out.

I caught Mr. Roth watching us from the corner of my eye. He had a satisfied look on his face. It pleased me somehow.

"Nurse Clayton and Miss Danes are right," Mr. Roth said. "You need to be more careful. Slow down when you eat ice cream, or anything, for that matter."

"I know. I'll be careful." She pouted when Mr. Roth put up his hand.

"No need to feel bad. You have done nothing wrong. We all love you." He went to Ellen and gave her a big hug, and her face lit up. "Why don't you take a nap before dinner?"

"I'll take her up," Sylvi said, putting her empty dish on the table. "We'll see you later."

Ellen hugged her uncle and waved to me. Sylvi took her hand as they went inside.

He turned to me. "What about you?"

"Oh, I'm fine. Just enjoying the beautiful garden."

"Today was great, wasn't it?"

"It was. I'm glad you came along."

His face lit up. "You are? I wasn't sure. You seem so tense in the theater."

"I wasn't tense." I gave him a confused look, hoping to dispel his correct assumption. "Ellen liked it. She wants to spend more time with you."

"Yes, I see that. But, my work . . . you know."

I tilted my head in understanding and we sat in silence, listening to the birds. I relaxed, enjoyed the peacefulness and perhaps I enjoyed him, too. My conflicting emotions confused me, but I put them out of my mind temporarily.

CHAPTER FIVE

A couple of weeks later at breakfast, Ellen was extra fidgety. "I'm going to be six soon," she said.

"You will. In two weeks," Mrs. Chambers said. "And you already know there is a big party for you. Extra fancy this year, I might say."

"That's right," I said.

Sylvi's face had a strange expression. "I knew it was in August. The twenty-ninth?"

"Uh-huh." Ellen's face beamed with delight looking around the table.

"I know someone born around the same date. Your Sun sign is Virgo."

Sylvi's smile looked forced, and I thought that odd.

"What's a sun sign?" Ellen said.

"It's the astrological sign for when you were born. Virgo is an earth sign. It means you are changeable, just like the Earth."

"Changeable? But I'm the same." Ellen resumed eating her toast and jam.

"You'll understand more when you are older."

"People always say that. Sure glad I'll be older soon."

We all laughed at her comment.

***

After Ellen's lessons were over, I went to Mrs. Chambers's office. She raised her head from a pile of mail. "May I help you, Miss Danes?"

"I hope so. It's a little embarrassing. I have nothing suitable to wear to Ellen's birthday party. Will it be formal?"

"Most of the lady guests dress up fairly fine."

"If I bought some fabric, is there a sewing machine I may borrow?"

"Most certainly. We have not only a machine, we have an entire sewing room."

"Where?"

"On the third floor on the east side, facing the sea. It's one of the locked doors. You might find some fabric there. Mrs. Roth senior kept a large store of fabrics. You may not have to buy anything.

"That would be great." I didn't want to admit it to Mrs. Chambers, but saving the expense on a dress I would probably only wear once eased my mind.

Mrs. Chambers led the way to the top floor, chatting away. "It was Mr. Roth's mother who loved to sew. She held monthly sewing circles here for the Ladies' Charity Society, and I was told they made clothes for the less than fortunate. We use the room now for mending clothes for the staff, Mr. Roth and Ellen, if needed. We keep it locked because it's a special room and Mr. Roth wants nothing, well, you know, disturbed."

She reached the door and stopped, removing a key ring from her belt, and unlocked the door. "It's dark in here." She went straight to the windows and opened the drapes. The room flooded with light.

"What a cheerful room," I said.

"It is. She must have loved color. It's everywhere."

Pale green walls with floral chintz curtains on the windows. Three sewing tables with ancient Singer sewing machines near the windows. A settee upholstered in the same floral chintz as the curtains and pillows piled high created a cozy sitting area on the opposite wall, including two Queen Ann arm chairs and an oval tea table.

"It's musty in here. I'll have the maids air it out and dust. The sewing machines are old, but they work fine. You know how to oil them?"

"I do," I said. Orpha's old machine was about the same age.

She walked to a wall of cupboards and opened several doors. "See? Look at all these wonderful materials. Something should suit your tastes."

Shelves were full of many types of fabrics, cotton duck, chintz in all colors, stripes, and florals, sateen, and my favorite, the elegant moire satin.

"Amazing." My hands fingered the shiny material in blue, pink, and gold. I loved how the light caught the swirls of pattern in the fabric.

"And in these drawers are patterns. Though most of them are outdated. If you're handy, you could modify them."

"Thank you so much."

"Don't thank me. Thank Mrs. Roth, rest her soul. I wish I had known her. Wonderful things have been said about her. She died young when Mr. Roth was a child. Very sad."

"Yes. I can relate."

"You too? Something you have in common." She gave me a sympathetic glance. "Well, here's an extra key. Just help yourself."

"I'll stay awhile and make some choices. Thanks again."

Hours passed without my realizing. It was fun going through all the fabrics and patterns. I found a pattern to modify into a modern style. I knew the fabric would be the right choice for me.

***

In the days leading up to Ellen's birthday, I learned there would be many guests invited along with the house staff to celebrate. They would present a big birthday cake with gifts from all the staff and, of course, Mr. Roth would shower her with gifts.

Mrs. Chambers said I didn't need to buy a gift. I had grown attached to Ellen, and I wanted to get her something. Ben drove me into town in the Bentley.

"Are you sure I must sit in the back seat?" Extremely uncomfortable with him driving me, I squirmed.

"Mr. Roth's orders. Enjoy it." He raised his eyes to the rear-view mirror.

I laughed out loud and relaxed, sprawling in the vehicle's luxuriousness.

When the car reached the gate, Ben pushed the button on the dash to open the gate and he steered the car onto the highway toward Plymouth.

I looked out the back window to watch the gate automatically close. Everything still held my awe.

He dropped me off at the local dime store, where I bought a wooden pencil box with a floral painted lid. I purchased colorful pencils to put in the box and some wrapping paper and a bow. I told Ben to give me an hour to browse the main street shops.

Strolling along Main Street, I noticed the Bentley parked in front of a café. Ben leaned into a woman with her back against the car. They smiled and laughed while talking. A twinge of jealousy ran through me. I wasn't interested in Ben, though I found him very attractive. Watching a couple acting as though they were in love, or at least in a relationship, triggered my fantasies of love. She could be someone walking down the street for all I knew. Ben flirted with anything in a skirt. He saw me and waved me over. The woman hurried away. I never saw her face.

"A girlfriend?" I teased.

"Just one of a million." He laughed, opening the door for me. I slid in while he shut my door and got into the driver's seat. "Find what you wanted for Ellen?"

"Yep."

I wondered about the woman. It was possible she was the person I saw in the courtyard. The rules were clear: no overnight guests on the estate.

"Does she work at the estate? I don't think I've seen her there."

"Nope. You sure are curious."

"Nope." I lied. Curiosity became my driving force. I was curious about the people of Rothmorton Hall.

The day of the birthday party had arrived, and the entire household was busy preparing for the guests, including children. There would also be Mr. Roth's business associates. It would have been strange with no children at a child's birthday party. Ellen was antsy and couldn't concentrate on her studies.

"Sit still and try reading the line again."

"Sorry Miss Danes, I'm excited 'bout the party."

"Understandable. You need to concentrate."

"Oh, all right." She heaved a sigh and frowned at the words, then carefully enunciated each word perfectly.

"Much better. See, you can do it when you try."

***

The afternoon moved at a snail's pace until three o'clock, when Sylvi arrived for Ellen to dress for the party.

"Excited about the party?" Sylvi asked.

"Are you kidding? Sure am. Aren't you?"

She giggled. "I'm dying to see all the bigwigs in their fancy clothes. What are you wearing?"

"It's a surprise."

"Good for you. I'll be wearing basic black. Good for all occasions, right?"

"Right. See you later," I said.

I'd never been to a big party like the Roth's and I worried about fitting in. The new dress I made hung on the handle of the wardrobe. Its blue satin shimmered in the lamplight, the full skirt and attached multi-layered tulle petticoat sticking out all fluffy, with a ballet neckline and elbow-length sleeves. I spent extra time on my hair sweeping it up in a French twist secured with rhinestone hair pins I found at the dime store in Plymouth, and took special care applying eyeliner, mascara, and a touch of eyeshadow I rarely wore.

When I stood in front of the full-length mirror, I gasped at my reflection, not recognizing myself. Pleased by my appearance, I applied red lipstick and pulled on the long white evening gloves I bought, especially for the dress. Smiling at myself, I wondered if Mr. Roth would approve. Then I frowned, thinking it didn't matter whether he approved, I approved. So there!

A knock on the door startled me. When I opened it, Ellen and Sylvi stood in fine dresses.

"Miss Danes, we came to get you. I want my two best friends to go down with me," Ellen said.

"How nice. You look lovely, dear. Turn around."

Ellen wore a new white dress with tiers of ruffled organza and a pink satin sash around her waist, lace-ruffled anklets and white patent Mary Jane shoes. She twirled around, making the full skirt float upward, then made a curtsy.

"How many petticoats are you wearing?" I asked.

"Five." Ellen giggled with glee.

"You look very nice too, Nurse Clayton, black suits your coloring," I said.

"It's a welcomed change from the uniform. What a gorgeous dress!" Sylvi said. "Ah, you were the one in the sewing room all week. I could hear the sewing machine going late into the night. It's right over my room."

"Hope it didn't disturb you."

"I read late."

"You look pretty." Ellen took my hand and Sylvi's too. I whispered a thank you in her ear as we went to the top of the main staircase and stopped.

"Are we ready?" Sylvi asked.

Loud voices drifted up the stairs, and my stomach tightened with nervousness again. We took the steps one by one, the staircase so wide we all could descend together, still holding hands.

"Ellen's coming down." Someone shouted.

The thunder of applause nearly deafened me as we reached the last step. Mr. Roth rushed to Ellen, scooping her up in his arms, her dress causing a flurry of fluff.

"Happy Birthday, my darling girl." He kissed her on the cheek and turned her around to display her to the crowd.

So thick with bodies I couldn't see through the crowd of hundreds. Ladies dressed in evening gowns and men in tuxes. Even Mr. Roth was wearing a tux, and I had never seen him with a tie. I couldn't take my eyes off him.

They set the Dining Room table up as an enormous buffet. Guests sat at strategically placed small linen-covered tables and chairs in the parlor and the Music Room. A string quartet played classical music, though the clamoring of voices canceled out most of it. The terrace doors were open and guests had overflowed outside where torches lit up the night. What a spectacle. The chandeliers sparkled and candles lit everywhere, along with enormous bouquets of flowers.

Sylvi had disappeared, so I wandered into the Dining Room. An unfamiliar waiter, one of the event staff, passed around trays of champagne and hors d'oeuvres. I took a glass and held it carefully, afraid to drink, for I was already giddy.

"You are stunning," said a man's voice. I spun around to Mr. Roth's face close to mine as the crowd made it impossible to stand far apart.

"Mr. Roth, I didn't see you. Thank you. Where's Ellen?"

"Probably with the children she knows."

"I thought you didn't entertain much."

"I don't, just Ellen's birthday."

"How thoughtful."

"Ellen is my world, couldn't you tell?"

"I suppose so." I muttered. My eyes were going cross-eyed, standing so close, and my heart was pounding.

"Let's go outside where it's less crowded."

I nodded and followed. He led the way, taking my hand. Once outside, I could breathe again. Another server passed by and Mr. Roth grabbed a glass of champagne, clinked mine and we both took sips.

"Cheers." He smiled at me warmly.

"This is some party. The scent of evening primrose smells divine too."

"Hm, you're wearing your hair different. Suits you."

"My, you are full of compliments tonight." His attention to my appearance made me happy and increased my inner conflict, vacillating back and forth about him, to stay or go. I kept telling myself it was Ellen. I didn't want to leave.

"And why not?" he said. "I'm in a great mood. Ellen's happy and she loves you."

"I love her too. She is a joy to be around. Easy to teach. Almost like not working."

"Oh, so I should cut your pay?"

"I wouldn't go so far." My laughter came effortlessly with him while we talked like old friends.

"Well, well, well. Who's this delightful creature we haven't had the pleasure of meeting?" An older gentleman and two women came up to us. The older of the two women must have been the man's wife and the younger pretty blond, mid-twenties, I assumed, was their daughter.

Mr. Roth shook the man's hand. "Jeeves, Martha, good to see you. And . . . of course, MaryLou," he nodded to the pretty young woman, then turned to me. "These are the Chabots, this is Miss Danes, our—"

"Do tell Miss Danes," MaryLou interrupted, "who's your designer?"

"My designer?"

"Simply love your dress." She spoke with an accent, as did the other two, possibly British.

"Thank you. I made this myself." I bit my lip. Probably shouldn't have admitted to making my own clothes. Too late. Both Martha and MaryLou raised their eyebrows, and it sure looked like Martha was looking down her nose at me. My throat went dry, and I glanced at Mr. Roth. He seemed oblivious to my discomfort.

MaryLou laughed, "You must be joking, surely. Tell me who designed it? Daddy had Christian Dior design this for me. Don't you love it?" She passed her hands down the front of her strapless gown with a very full tulle skirt.

"It's beautiful," I said.

"Oh MaryLou, don't be silly," said Martha. "Of course, she doesn't have a designer. She's Ellen's new nanny. Aren't you dear?" Martha said, eying me through a monocle.

The tone she used made me want to shrivel up and disappear. Then I remembered the monocle was out of style, since the first world war. I smothered a laugh and took a sip of champagne, feeling much better.

"She's not a nanny," Mr. Roth said. "She's a teacher I hired to tutor Ellen."

"Isn't it the same thing?" Jeeves asked.

"Uh, not exactly. You know my mother sewed up a storm making all kinds of clothing." Mr. Roth gave a look of pride.

"I remember. She led the Ladies Charity Society," Martha said.

MaryLou turned to Mr. Roth, fluttering her eyelashes and cooed. "Oh Hugh, how is your new Roadster? Don't you remember you promised to take me for a spin?" She threaded her arm through his and shimmied in close to his side.

Just when I thought Mr. Roth should have backed me up more strongly, the possibility threw me that MaryLou and Mr. Roth could be an item.

His mouth dropped open for a second. "Uh, did I? I suppose we could sometime."

"You better. And what about the Kennedy wedding? You better not be taking someone other than me." She hugged his arm a little tighter.

"That's right," said Jeeves. "John Kennedy has a brilliant future as the new senator. We wouldn't miss his wedding to the lovely Jackie."

"You are attending?" Martha asked, her eyebrows arching.

Mr. Roth cleared his throat. "Uh, I've forgotten all about it. There's been a lot going on lately."

MaryLou gave him a jab in the arm. "Forgot? How could you forget the event of the season? I wondered why you hadn't asked me. It's in less than two weeks, September 12, you simply must R.S.V.P."

"You know the Kennedy's?" I asked Mr. Roth. I knew very little about them, but I read the local papers and John Kennedy was definitely someone important, particularly in the area.

He gave me an embarrassed nod, then faced the Chabots. "I'm sorry, but I don't think I'll be going. It's too late to R.S.V.P. now anyway."

"True," Martha said with a frown.

"How very disappointing," MaryLou said, pulling her arm from Mr. Roth's.

If Mr. Roth was embarrassed, I was even more out of place in the conversation. Turning to leave, Ellen pushed her way through the crowd.

"Uncle Hugh?" Ellen was dragging a little girl with her. "Kathy wants to know when we eat cake, and when I open presents?"

The Chabots took the hint and moved on to join another group of guests. The entire scene with them sent my self-confidence into a tailspin. I turned my attention to Ellen and Kathy.

"Oh, Kathy wants to know?" Mr. Roth chuckled. "After people eat, then we will announce the cake. Okay?" He patted the top of her head.

Kathy laughed along with Ellen as they skipped off together, back through the crowd.

"Hungry?" Mr. Roth took my arm and flashed me a brilliant smile.

"Definitely." Struggling with feelings of inadequacy and whether Mr. Roth and MaryLou were a thing, I wanted to be somewhere else.

We waded through the throngs of guests into the Dining Room. We made plates together and took a seat at a small table in the parlor. I pulled off the fingers of the long gloves and tucked them into the wrist opening before diving into the sumptuous meal.

Several couples came up to us and Mr. Roth introduced me as Miss Danes, not the tutor. He was courteous and a charming host. After we finished eating, Mr. Roth became absorbed into a business discussion with an associate when I noticed Mrs. Chambers waving me over to where she was standing, so I went to see what she wanted.

"Are you having fun, Miss Danes?"

"I am. It's a wonderful party."

"Your dress came out beautifully. You fit right in."

Once again, my issue of fitting in slammed into my face. Before I could reply, she turned to instruct a waiter on some issue and I found myself alone. I had almost put the incident with the Chabots aside. All it took was Mrs. Chambers' comment to knock me down. For a short time, I blended in with the crowd. Mr. Roth's compliments were welcomed and, for a few moments, I actually enjoyed his company. However, it was clear Mrs. Chambers viewed me as the help and I was—after all. My urge to run away was overwhelming, and before I did something impulsive, I had to talk to Mr. Roth.

Before I knew it, two kitchen staff carried in the cake. The enormous multi-tiered monstrosity with a large sparkly number six candle sitting on the top layer was placed on a special table in the corner, next to a mountain of gifts. The candle was lit, and the lights dimmed while Mr. Roth carried Ellen to the cake so she could blow out the candle. Everyone sang the "Happy Birthday" song and Ellen clapped her hands, grinning ear to ear.

While Ellen opened gifts, Mrs. Chambers took notes on who they were from. Guests trickled out the door, leaving just the staff and Mr. Roth sitting around Ellen, exclaiming over each gift. When she came to mine, she jumped up and ran into my arms and kissed my cheek.

"Oh, Miss Danes, thank you, thank you," Ellen said.

"I'm glad you like it." I gave her a brief hug.

She ran back to finish opening gifts. It touched me to the core at her display of affection in front of everyone. I shot a sidelong glance at Mr. Roth, and he gave me a nod of approval. All it took for me to forget Mrs. Chambers's words about my fitting in. His acceptance was all I needed.

When Ellen had fallen asleep in her uncle's arms, he carried her up the stairs, followed by Sylvi and me. I watched at the door while they readied her for bed, still asleep, and tucked in. Mr. Roth kissed her forehead and met me out in the hall.

"Glad you're still here. Let me walk you to your room. I want to ask you something."

We strolled down the hallway to my room. I said nothing, waiting.

"Tomorrow, I'm taking Ellen, and of course Nurse Clayton will attend to Cape Cod for a day on the yacht. I want you to come too."

"Me? Are you sure?"

"Of course. It's part of Ellen's birthday."

"There's something we need to discuss."

He tilted his head and made that crooked smile of his. "Now?"

"I think so." I walked to the end of the hall by the round window, not wanting our voices to be heard by Ellen, in case she was still awake. He followed me.

"What is this about?" He was obviously clueless.

"I've been unhappy and considering resigning and going back to Illinois." I avoided his gaze, shocked at how the words tumbled from my mouth.

"You must be joking. Why on earth are you unhappy?"

I looked up and saw his disbelief. "It's your attitude toward me. The teasing and the insults. Please stop or I can't work for you anymore."

His face fell, and he shoved his hands in his pockets. "Oh, I see. I'm so very sorry I've insulted you and yes, I tease you."

"Don't you think it's unprofessional, considering our employer - employee relationship?"

"When you look at it that way, I agree. I've been inappropriate. Though in my defense, it's because I feel so comfortable around you."

I took that surprising comment in, but continued on. "I've been angry with you and it's affected my attitude toward this job."

"So, you would leave me . . . uh, Rothmorton and Ellen?"

"Only if we can't come to an agreement. I love Ellen and want to give her the best of my abilities without feeling inadequate."

"Oh, Miss Danes, you are not inadequate in any way, trust me. Look, I promise to stop with the teasing and inappropriate behavior. Please stay. Ellen needs you, and I want you to stay."

He was being genuine. It showed all over his face. I wanted to believe him and I wanted to stay. After a few tense moments, I sighed with relief.

"Thank you, Mr. Roth, for listening."

"So, you'll stay? And go with us tomorrow on the yacht?"

"I'll stay and I'd love to go on the yacht."

"Great! We'll leave at the front entrance after breakfast."

We returned to my door, and he gave me a slight bow and strode away down the hall.

My heart was pounding from the confrontation. I had only done something like that with Orpha. I was proud of myself for saying what I felt and wanted from him. Positive I did the right thing and relaxed. I wondered if I would have left? It didn't matter, because Mr. Roth and I had an agreement.

A day yachting on the Cape would be exciting.

CHAPTER SIX

At breakfast, everyone moved slower and quieter than usual and I arrived later than usual. The rest of the staff must have partied long after I retired. Needing more caffeine, I lingered for an extra cup of coffee after everyone, except Mrs. Chambers, went back to their duties.

"Did you enjoy the party?" she said.

"It was magical, especially for Ellen."

"She sure loves a party."

"She wasn't at breakfast with Nurse Clayton."

"Ellen slept in and I had their breakfast sent up. She has a long day ahead."

"Yes, I'm excited about it." I paused, taking another sip of my coffee. "I was wondering . . . is it usual for a child Ellen's age spending so much time with the staff?"

"Not on any of the estates I've worked. It's different here, for sure. Mr. Roth doesn't want Ellen to be alone, or just with her nurse. He wants to surround her with people. I'm sure for companionship, and also, he wants her to understand the differences in people. I find it admirable."

"Really. How interesting," I said.

Mrs. Chambers stopped and became solemn. "He must have had a very lonely childhood. I mean, caring so much to make Ellen's different."

"Possibly." My heart hurt for Mr. Roth, as it hurt for my childhood. It was the moment I realized, despite my threats to leave, my feelings for Mr.

Roth ran much deeper than I had originally thought. How did I not know? Maybe that was the real reason I was so upset and insulted by Mr. Roth's behavior towards me. I thought he didn't like me and now I wanted him to. But I had set a precedent, that our relationship was purely professional. How do I deal with these newly discovered feelings? Thoroughly confused, I pushed the thoughts aside and went to Sylvi's room to see if she was ready for our yachting trip.

Before I knocked, I heard her talking on the phone, her voice elevated and agitated.

"I haven't found out anything yet, I tell you. Stop pushing . . . I know how long I've been here. I'll call you when I have more information . . . Well, I know one thing's for sure, Hugh is hiding something. I'll find out if it's the last thing I do." She slammed down the receiver.

Stunned, I took a step back. What was she talking about and why did she call Mr. Roth, Hugh? I waited a moment, then knocked.

Sylvi opened the door, and I smiled hello and we collected Ellen from her room and I acted like I hadn't heard a thing. Something was definitely off and my suspicions about her returned.

Ben was out front with the limousine and we all climbed in. Ellen jumped into the seat just behind Ben, who closed the glass sliding window between him and the rest of us. Sylvi, Mr. Roth, and I slid into the large seat behind Ellen. It was cozy. Yet plenty of room for us three. Ellen did most of the talking in her delightful way. By the time she finished her story, we had arrived. Ben parked the limousine at the entrance to the dock at the Barnstable pier in Cape Cod Bay.

"There she is!" Ellen pointed to an incredibly long yacht with towering masts and several crew on board. One of them, wearing what I assumed was a captain's uniform with gold braid on his navy-blue jacket, stood waiting at the ramp to the yacht.

Once again, Mr. Roth's wealth impressed me. The yacht hailed both sails and engine power. Ellen and Sylvi rushed up the ramp and into a luxurious lounge paneled in dark woods polished to a high luster and a bar with swivel stools. The two settled themselves on the long sofa.

Mr. Roth pulled me aside. "Would you like to see the bridge?"

"What's the bridge?"

"Where they steer the yacht."

"Oh, yes, I would love to." My ignorance was difficult to hide, but he was very polite and guided me up the steps.

He gave a brief introduction of me to the captain, then explained all the various pieces of navigation equipment. The engines roared. I jolted from the movement as it backed out of the dock and into the bay.

"Oh, what a fabulous view from here." I gazed out the large glass window.

"It really is the best place to see it. Nothing in the way." Mr. Roth beamed with pride. "We don't want to be a nuisance while they are busy. Let's move on."

I followed him down the steps again on the other side. He pointed to some steps that went below.

"On the lower deck are the staterooms for overnight trips. We haven't done that in a long time. Something to plan, I suppose. Let's go watch as we head into the open sea."

Outside the lounge, I leaned on the rail, looking at the water rush against the sides of the boat. They raised the sails, and the wind whipped through my loose hair, sending it flying every which way. I took a head band from my jacket pocket and pulled my hair out of my face.

"Isn't it wonderful to be on the water?" Mr. Roth came up next to me and leaned on the rail.

"My first time."

"Really? Well, I am honored to host your first voyage."

I didn't detect a note of sarcasm in his voice at all. His sincerity continued to baffle me. I expected a wealthy man like him to be posh, arrogant, and haughty. Like the Chabots. Mr. Roth was the exact opposite.

"Has anyone ever told you, Miss Danes, you have Bette Davis eyes? I mean, when she was younger. You are much better looking. I hope you don't mind the compliment."

Even in the cool wind, I blushed. "I've heard it once or twice, however, I don't see it. I accept your compliment." My mouth was spreading into a broad smile against my will.

"There it is. Your fabulous smile, and I love it when you blush. It adds the perfect amount of color to your cheeks."

"Watch it. I think you're flirting."

"Sorry. I promised I wouldn't be inappropriate, didn't I?" His eyes twinkled in the light.

My stomach filled with butterflies, which baffled me more. "May I ask you something?"

"I think you just did." He winked at me.

"Very funny. Some people at the party talked with a British accent. Are they from England?"

He chuckled. "Maybe one or two. I think what you are referring to is called the mid-Atlantic talk. Those who have money talk that way."

"You have money. You don't talk like that."

"Used to, until I went into the service. I wanted to fit in. Not sound like a snob. So I lost it."

"I'm glad you don't sound like a snob." It surprised me he also wanted to fit in.

"I must apologize for the Chabots, though. They were impossibly rude to you."

"Forget it. I did." He didn't look convinced, so I turned my attention to the ocean.

"I should have been clear with Jeeves. That was my error."

I glanced his way just as he frowned and stared out at the ocean. "The Kennedy wedding. Sounds like a very important event. MaryLou was very disappointed you didn't ask her to be your date."

He laughed. "MaryLou and I have known each other since she was a baby. She's a big flirt, but I don't take her seriously. She's much too young. Hasn't even graduated high school yet."

"Really? She looks so mature. The designer dress and hair."

He eyed me curiously. "Would it bother you if I was interested in MaryLou?"

"Now that I know her age, yes. Otherwise, it's really none of my business what you do in your personal life. I shouldn't have pried." Relief ran through me. I was wrong about the two of them. Despite our agreement, he continued to tease a little, and I was growing more disappointed I had confronted him.

The yacht had moved further out of the bay and a rolling wave caused it to tilt. I fell sideways into him and he put his hand on my arm to steady me. A delicious tingling ran up my arm. Our eyes locked. When I tore my eyes away, I could sense his gaze on me. What was happening to me? I detested him, didn't I?

Ellen's laughter floated over the air from inside the lounge. "You cheat, Nurse Clayton." More laughter from the two of them. Mr. Roth and I went back inside to join them. Disappointed, I wanted to stay on the deck with him.

Ellen left the card table and joined me and Mr. Roth on the sofa, sitting right between us. I thought it was cute.

"Uncle Hugh, where are my mommy and daddy?"

Mr. Roth inhaled sharply, sending me strange signals. His jaw jutted as he licked his lips. Why was he hesitating?

"I've told you many times. Why are you asking?"

"One of my friends asked me at my party. I didn't know what to say."

"What did you tell her, sweetheart?" Mr. Roth looked at Sylvi and then at me as if he were nervous.

"They were gone. Where did they go?"

"In Heaven, honey." He patted her hand. "Remember?"

"Where is Heaven? I forget."

Mr. Roth pointed upward. "Up there somewhere beyond the clouds. No one living can go there. So, we don't know exactly where it is."

"Oh. Why did they go there?"

He rubbed his neck and twisted his mouth like he wasn't sure what he should say. "I told you. There was an accident. They couldn't take care of you, so I did."

"Okay."

"Aren't you glad I did?"

"Yes, I love you, Uncle Hugh." Ellen wrapped her little arms around him tight and kissed his cheek and he kissed hers.

A sigh a relief came from him and I shot a glance at Sylvi. She had a strange look on her face I couldn't read. The mood had changed, and I was uncomfortable.

"Let's go out on deck and watch the seagulls flying overhead," I said.

Ellen jumped up and clapped her hands together with glee. "How fun, let's go." She grabbed my hand and rushed out the door to the deck.

Seagulls were flying over the yacht at the rear. Ellen ran, and I tried to keep up.

"Don't run Ellen," shouted Mr. Roth, who had followed us outside.

Ellen slowed as I caught up with her. "Button up your sweater, Ellen. It's colder out here."

She ignored me. Her attention focused on the birds. "Look, look at them." She shouted, jumping up and down.

"Here, let me," I said, turning her around, struggling to button her up, but she wouldn't stop jumping. She was too excited.

When suddenly, Ellen made a horrible sound.

"She's wheezing." Sylvi rushed to Ellen, getting down on her knees in front of her. "Okay Ellen, calm yourself."

Mr. Roth rushed to Ellen's side. "Let's get her back inside. It must be the cold wind and her excitement." He lifted her into his arms, carrying her into the lounge.

Ellen continued the horrendous wheezing as he laid her on the sofa. "Ellen, just calm down. Don't let this scare you like the other times, okay? Nurse Clayton will get the inhaler to help you breathe if you need it."

Not knowing how to help, I waited. Ellen continued to wheeze, and it only got worse. Sylvi got her medical bag from the table and rummaged through it. She pulled everything out of the bag onto the table. Something was wrong.

"Nurse Clayton, where is the damn contraption?" He tried to keep his voice low and calm. There was unmistakable tension in his voice. He seemed frightened, too.

"I'm sorry, Mr. Roth, the adrenalin for the inhaler isn't in my medical bag. I checked it the other day and everything was there.

"What do you mean, it's not in your bag?" Mr. Roth said.

"Someone must have taken it. Doesn't seem possible. It's just not here."
She continued to rummage through her bag, her face clearly distressed.

"Someone?" I asked, then bit my lip. Why would someone put Ellen's
life in jeopardy? The scene before me became twisted into one of
desperation and fear.

"It's unacceptable. What's the point of having one if it's not here when
we need it?" Mr. Roth's voice elevated. "This was your responsibility,
Nurse Clayton, to be available for emergencies such as this. I'm holding you
personally responsible if anything happens."

Sylvi sat motionless at his words, her face ashen.

I could hold my tongue no longer and whispered. "Mr. Roth, please,
you are upsetting Ellen."

Everyone turned to Ellen, whose wheezing had intensified with tears
welling up in her frightened eyes.

"Ellen, my dearest, I'm sorry I raised my voice. There, there." Mr. Roth
sat beside her and stroked her hair and kissed her cheek.

"We need to take her to the hospital, Mr. Roth," Sylvi said.

"What can I do?" I stepped forward.

"Just stay out of the way," Mr. Roth said, his voice a terse whisper. He
shouted to a steward standing near the door. "Tell the captain to turn this
damn boat around. Get us back to the docks as fast as possible. Use the
engines."

The steward shot down the deck and hollered, "Drop Sails!" and ran
up the step to the bridge to inform the Captain of Mr. Roth's instructions.
I heard the sails collapsing as the engine revved up and vibrated beneath my
feet. As the yacht turned, we all swayed. I almost fell over and plopped into
the nearest seat.

Mr. Roth was worried and angry, and I understood. The way he spoke
to me, though, hurt. I stifled my feelings because Ellen was the important
focus, not my ego.

"Un . . . cle, H-Hugh, I'm s-scared." She struggled between wheezes.

"Relax, pumpkin. You'll be fine as soon as we get you to the hospital."
He patted her small hand, forcing a smile.

I started to leave the cabin when Ellen reached out to me.

"D-don't go."

My heart stopped at her pleading voice and rushed to her, taking her hand. I motioned to Sylvi to join us and the three of us surrounded the frightened Ellen until her wheezing slowed. We all knew she still needed the hospital.

The yacht reached the dock in record time. Mr. Roth carried Ellen to the limousine. Ben was waiting. The captain must have radioed him. All in, Ben hit the accelerator, and it was fifteen minutes to the hospital in Hyannis, a three-story white house with a red-shingled roof. Mr. Roth and Sylvi went to the emergency area with Ellen. A nurse directed me to a waiting room.

I agonized over Ellen's condition. It was heart-rending to see her in such distress. I wrung my hands and paced the floor until Sylvi came in.

"Mr. Roth is staying and said for us to return to Rothmorton with Ben. There's nothing we can do while Ellen is being stabilized. This isn't her first crisis."

"How long will she be here?"

"A few days, maybe more, depending on her recovery."

"The poor child."

Sylvi nodded as we left the hospital. Ben was leaning against the hood. When he saw us, he stood at attention, then opened the car door. "She gonna be okay?" he said.

"We hope so," Sylvi said.

***

Mr. Roth had stayed two nights at the hospital in Ellen's room. The hospital rarely allowed it. In Ellen's case, having her uncle present comforted her, especially since they tented her with oxygen.

When Sylvi and I arrived to visit Ellen, Mr. Roth went back with Ben to freshen up and take a nap. Mr. Roth said he would drive to the hospital in the Roadster.

It was the first I'd seen Ellen since the day we brought her in. Sylvi went straight for Ellen, giving her a hug and sat in the chair next to her bed.

"H-Hello," Ellen said, her voice weak.

"Don't talk, you've just been taken off oxygen, so we'll do the talking," Sylvi said, smiling. "We are very happy to see you. We've missed you very much."

I pulled up an extra chair and sat on the other side of Ellen's bed. "You bet we've missed you. I don't have anyone to force to read." I chuckled, trying to keep things upbeat. Ellen's face was pale and her curls flattened.

She tried to laugh, but nothing came. Her usual smiling self looked tired. "I . . . I'm sorry," Ellen said.

"It's not your fault, honey," Sylvi said, patting her little hand. "Have they been good to you here? Just nod your head."

"Uh-huh, not as . . . nice as you," Ellen said, managing a weak smile. "I want to go home."

"When you get stronger, you'll be home soon. A few more days. We don't want you to have a relapse," Sylvi said.

"Try not to talk," I said. "It was nice your uncle stayed here every day for you. He loves you very much?"

Ellen nodded her head. "I l-love h-him." Her breathing grew slower.

I thought she might cry, and I put my hand over my heart as it tightened at how lonely she must be, surrounded by strangers. It brought back my time in the institution infirmary for my tonsils. So young and alone. I was miserable.

"Everyone at home wishes you a speedy recovery and they all miss you." Sylvi and I gave each other a hopeful glance.

The nurse took Ellen's vitals and left. We tried cheering her up with funny stories and how the staff missed her and thinking of her. It did little good. She barely laughed or smiled, though laughing wasn't good for her.

A couple of hours later, Ben picked us up.

In the car, I drew a hanky from my bag and dabbed my eyes. "Sorry, I know Ellen is progressing. My heart breaks to see her suffer."

She reached over and squeezed my hand. "I feel the same, Dee. She is so young and treatments have improved little in the past fifty years. I'm glad you are here for her. I can tell she loves you."

"She loves you too, Sylvi." It was a tender moment between us and the closeness to Sylvi returned. I wanted her friendship and our fears for Ellen connected us. I put the phone conversation I overheard out of my mind for the time being.

When we arrived at the estate, a police car was at the front entrance and behind it a tow truck with Mr. Roth's roadster hooked up to it.

"Mr. Roth was in an accident?" My heart lurched at the thought of him being hurt. This couldn't be happening.

"I hope he's all right. I'll get my bag from upstairs," said Sylvi.

Ben stopped at the front. Sylvi and I hurried inside. I rushed on ahead into the parlor to find Mr. Roth sitting on the settee with a bandage on his forehead, fussing with Mrs. Chambers. Relief flooded through me. He was all right.

"I'm fine, Mrs. Chambers. I don't need a doctor. If I need one, I'll ask at the hospital when I get there."

"Let me look." Sylvi breathed heavily and went to Mr. Roth's side to check his head, then opened her bag to retrieve some supplies. He tried to push her away.

"Mr. Roth, please let Sylvi help you. You are useless to Ellen if you're hurt." I moved toward him.

He glanced at me, paused for a moment, then nodded to Sylvi, allowing her to examine him.

"Just a few bruises and another scratch. The bandage Mrs. Chambers had applied looks good," Sylvi said. "You'll be sore though by tomorrow. If you need anything for pain, here's some aspirin." She put a small bottle in his palm.

"Thanks, Nurse Clayton. I'm glad we have you around." He gritted a smile, though he didn't apologize for speaking to her so harshly on the yacht.

The inspector finished writing his report. "I'm done for now, Mr. Roth. I'll give you a report once we run the prints." He tipped his hat and left.

Ben was standing near the doorway, looking concerned.

Mr. Roth raised his eyes to our concerned faces. "I'm fine. The brakes gave out, and I crashed."

"Impossible," Ben said. "I checked the car out yesterday. The brakes were in perfect condition."

"I'm sure you did, Ben. The tow truck driver said they were cut," Mr. Roth said.

"Cut?" My shocked voice was a bit too loud.

"That's crazy, man. What did the police say?" Ben looked floored.

"They dusted for prints and will get back to me."

Everyone was worried, including me, and I realized something very sinister was going on.

"Ben, I need you to take me to the hospital to see Ellen." Mr. Roth stood.

"Right. You shouldn't be driving," Sylvi said. "Get checked out in the ER to make sure you don't have a concussion. The gash is still oozing. I've cleaned it up for now. Mrs. Chambers, you did well in a cinch."

"I'm no nurse, for sure. Glad I could help." Mrs. Chambers took her leave.

"Sure you're all right," I asked.

"Definitely." He gave me an encouraging smile. "Thanks for being concerned, uh, all of you. I promise to have a doctor look at me. I need to change my shirt again. Ben, give me a few and I'll meet you outside."

Everyone left the room, leaving me with Mr. Roth. "I'm so worried. Ellen would be devastated if anything happened to you."

"I'm fine. How was your visit with Ellen?"

"She's so weak, broke my heart."

"I know. This isn't her first hospital stay. She's a trooper."

"So are you."

We stood so close the warmth of his breath passed over my lips. He saw my concern and I could see he was trying hard not to show his. That someone tried to kill him hit me at my core and I couldn't ignore it. Who would want to hurt him and Ellen?

CHAPTER SEVEN

On my day off, Ben drove me into Plymouth to spend the day. After window shopping, I stopped at the café taking a seat by the window. I liked to people watch. A couple walking arm-in-arm passed my window and across the street stood a family of four in front of the ice cream parlor, laughing and eating ice cream cones. Despite myself, I longed for those experiences and my mind wandered to thoughts of Mr. Roth.

"I haven't seen you in here before. You new to the area?" The waitress interrupted my people-watching. She seemed extra friendly.

"Oh, hello. I didn't notice you there. Since August, I have been here. I'm from Illinois."

"Me too. Since July, from up north. I'm Becky." She tapped her name tag with her pen.

"Hi Becky, I'll have the blue plate special and a cup of coffee with cream."

"Sure thing." She finished writing up the ticket and stuck her pen into her pale bleach-blond curls showing almost an inch of dark growth. She had beautifully manicured nails, and I wondered how she managed working as a waitress. I recalled the first day Ben drove to town. He had been talking to a woman. I wondered if it was her. Becky was mature, maybe forty, and I thought too old for Ben.

Becky went to place my order, and I gazed out the window. Ben was to pick me up in a couple of hours. He was still in town, half-way down the block, talking to a young woman. Of course he was. What a flirt. I pondered at how many women he knew in town.

"Here you go," Becky said.

"That was fast."

"The specials usually are." She placed the plate in front of me with one hand while pouring coffee with the other. "You work at a mansion around here?"

"I do."

"Which one? If you don't mind my askin'. I heard Rothmorton Estates was hiring for a new maid. You know anything about them?"

"I didn't know they were hiring. I'm the tutor there."

"No kiddin'. I heard some gossip about that Mr. Roth. He's quite the catch, even though he was married."

I choked on my sandwich. "Married?"

"Oh, not now, in the past. Didn't you know?"

"I understood he was unmarried."

"Secrets in the manor?" she laughed. "Just kidding. You stop by anytime, even just for a coffee. I don't know a lot of single women here, assuming you are single, no ring. You know what I mean?"

"Right, no ring. I'll stop by. Not a lot of places in town for lunch."

I had a hard time understanding why no one mentioned Mr. Roth had been married before, and I wanted to ask Mrs. Chambers about it.

After lunch, I browse the shop windows some more, stopping in the small bookshop and purchased the bestseller, *From Here to Eternity*. I had read about the film version being released but not yet showing.

I found Ben leaning up against the wall of the theater, smoking a cigarette. When he saw me, he extinguished the butt on the ground and put his hat back on. I slipped into the back seat. He took his place in the driver's seat and we headed back to Rothmorton.

"How'd your day go?" He glanced at me through the rear-view mirror.

"Good. I might have made a new friend. The waitress at the café. She seemed nice. You know her?"

"Who?"

"Becky, the blond. I figured you knew all the single women in town." I chuckled.

He raised a brow. "Oh, the older broad? Not my type. Yeah, she can sure talk your ear off." He laughed.

"She mentioned Rothmorton was hiring for a maid. Sounds like she's looking to change jobs."

"I hadn't heard. I'm not told about openings until they show up at the gate." He threw me a wink.

"Ha, ha, hilarious." Satisfied, Becky wasn't one of Ben's girls. Would be weird for me getting friendly with someone involved with him.

***

Ellen was due home the next day, and I wanted to speak to Mrs. Chambers before the house was full of excitement. She had her back to me, pouring herself a cup of tea. I knocked lightly on the open door.

"If you're not busy, I have some questions."

She turned around and waved me in. "Of course, dearie. What is it?" She was always cheerful.

Closing the door, I took the seat in front of her desk.

"You look serious. Something else happen?"

"Not exactly. I heard some things in town about Mr. Roth."

"Just town gossip, no doubt."

"Possibly. Was Mr. Roth married before?"

"Didn't I explain it to you when you first came?"

"Explain what?"

"Oh dear, I must apologize. It's because Mr. Roth hired you directly through the mail. Usually, I'm involved. Simply forgot."

I looked at her expectantly.

"Mr. Roth forbids anyone to discuss his former wife. Especially to Ellen."

"Why? What happened to her?"

"I've been told they annulled the marriage. The woman left. Must have been painful for Mr. Roth. Not wanting things said in his house. We can't control what the folks in town talk about."

"When did all this happen?"

"Before I came to work here. Maybe seven or eight years ago."

"Okay, I appreciate you filling me in. Don't you find it strange?"

"It's not for me or for you to question, now, is it? Just forget about it and do your job. It's what I do." She smiled and looked at some papers on her desk, sending the message I was dismissed.

It all seemed strange. What could have happened to Mr. Roth's marriage? Did he do something to make her leave? Despite all his teasing and insults, he was an affable man and showers love on Ellen. It was just difficult to understand. If he is still so upset by the annulment, it must have been something his wife did. Was he was still in love with her? If that's the case, it's all the better I kept our interaction strictly professional. But I was very curious, indeed.

I exited the back door, heading for the garden to take my daily walk. As I passed through the courtyard, Ben was outside working on an automobile. He waved me over.

"Everything ready for Ellen's return tomorrow?" he said.

"Yep, and everyone will be very relieved she's better. You've certainly been busy. With all the trips to the hospital and for me." I leaned against one of the other cars while he worked.

"It's my job, after all." He winked and laughed, prying something out of the engine.

"And you love it, I can tell. What the heck is that thing?"

"A carburetor." He held it up.

"Oh." I enjoyed talking to Ben. It was easy to talk with him. Like the brother I never had. "I'm off for my walk. See you tomorrow at breakfast." I smiled at him and turned toward the mansion when I noticed someone standing at the large round window on the second floor. It was Mr. Roth watching me. I waved, and he simply nodded. Maybe he was checking to make sure Ellen's room was ready for her. Thinking nothing more about it, I made my way through the courtyard to the garden gate entrance.

Passing the windows of the morning room, Mr. Roth came out its patio door. He must have dashed down the backstairs.

"Were you checking on Ellen's room? I'm sure Sylvi has everything set up for her."

"She does. I wanted to talk to you."

"Can we talk while I walk? Need to stretch my legs."

He nodded as we moved along the garden path. There was an awkward silence, making me wonder why he had said nothing. A few minutes passed when he stopped. "I just wanted to warn you about Ben."

"Ben? What do you mean?"

He shoved his hands deep into the pockets of his pants. A habit of his, when something was on his mind.

"He's a-a womanizer."

I chuckled. "I've gathered as much. He's a flirt, and I don't think it's a secret."

"I've known him a long time. We served in the war. I know how he can be." He gave me a serious look.

"Not with me. He's being friendly, and I enjoy his company."

"Well, I don't like it."

"I don't understand. Are you telling me not to talk to him?" I stopped walking, and the hairs raised on my neck like a cat.

"Not exactly. It's just—" He stopped walking too.

"Don't worry about me. I promise not to be taken in by Ben's charms if you're worried about it." My tone was curt.

He looked away, as if embarrassed. "Something like that."

The conversation confused me. He acted like a jealous boyfriend. Which made little sense, if he was still in love with his ex-wife. The whole situation was ludicrous.

"I appreciate your concern, Mr. Roth." I resumed my walk alone, hurrying ahead, turning just enough to catch him in my peripheral. He was standing there observing me.

I left the garden and reached the path along the cliffs, and paused at the railing. He had me thoroughly confused. On the yacht, it was so relaxing and comfortable with him. Until now. I questioned his actions. He was getting too personal. He didn't have the right to control who I talked to. Orpha would tell me who my friends should be and I hated it. My independence was hard won. The more I thought about it, the more my anger grew.

Then again, he may be overprotective. Like he was with Ellen. Shouldn't I feel good about it? The problem was, I didn't want his kind of protection. He was trying to manipulate me. Wasn't that what he accused Ben of doing?

"Miss Danes." Mr. Roth had followed me. "I want to apologize again." With furrowed brows, he reached for my hand, but I stepped back.

"You are concerned. I can see now." Because he came after me, my anger waned.

"My methods aren't always perfect." He gave a sheepish grin and leaned back against the rail when it moved and broke free. He fell backward toward the cliff's edge.

"Mr. Roth!" I lunged for him, grabbing his arm as it swung out wildly. The rail landed on the ground with him and me sprawled just inches from the edge. I yelped as my left hand hit the gravel. He rolled the both of us toward the path and away from the cliff.

"My God, are you alright?" His eyes were wide.

"Are you?" I heaved breathlessly. Our noses barely touched when I realized I was on top of him.

He didn't move, holding me fast. "I'm fine."

Embarrassed, I pushed myself off and sat up.

"You're shaking. There's a hole in the knee of your pants." He leaned toward my knee.

Blood spread through the fabric. "It doesn't hurt, probably just a scratch. You fell on the rail. Does your back hurt?"

"I'll have a bruise, but I'm not injured. You saved my life, you know, by grabbing my arm. I might have gone right over." He helped me up and gazed into my eyes. "I'm forever grateful."

"It was instinct. I'm sure your life wasn't in danger, Mr. Roth." My mouth had gone dry, thinking he might have died, and possibly me along with him.

"Well, I'm sure. Look how close we were."

I looked down and nearly swooned when I saw how close we were to the edge. I took a step back, holding onto his arm. "Oh my. You're right."

"I wasn't paying attention. Shouldn't have leaned against it. This railing has been here for decades." He turned to inspect the railing. "The post came right out. Should never have happened."

"I walk along here nearly every day. Never noticed it loose." I brushed off some dirt from my pants.

"See the base of the post? There are dig marks and these deep scratches." He ran his hand through his hair.

"You mean someone did this on purpose?"

"I guess we'll need to put this on our growing list of strange happenings. I'll have this path blocked on both ends until it's fixed."

"Good idea. Oh, and Mr. Roth, I accept."

"What?"

"Your apology."

I managed a strained smile while he took my hand to steady me and I leaned into him as we left the cliff.

***

When Ellen came home from the hospital, we all fussed over her. She sure enjoyed the attention. I stood in the background observing, not wanting to impede her homecoming, which didn't last long, since Mr. Roth took her straight to bed as the staff welcomed her along the way. Sylvi and I followed behind them.

"Is she really recovered?" I asked Sylvi.

"Not completely. She's well enough to be home. I can care for her now. She's a trooper."

"She is. You go on ahead. I'll come back later, after Ellen is all settled in. Too many people would overwhelm her."

I hadn't been in the classroom since they admitted Ellen to the hospital. I needed to set up for when she was ready to start lessons again. What I found when I opened the door shocked and saddened me. The room was in shambles. Books scattered over the floor with pages torn from the spines. Desks turned over on their sides, including my desk, and notebooks torn with heavy red pen marks across my writing. What appalled me even more were the words scrawled across the blackboard. It gave me a chill, sending goosebumps down my arms.

THE WORST IS YET TO COME!

Turning in circles, I stared, aghast, at the damage. Was this meant for me? Or Ellen? I remembered the cat on my first day, then the missing adrenalin, now this? But the cut brakes causing Mr. Roth's accident were clearly meant for him. It made little sense.

I tried the intercom. No answer. Frustrated, I rushed from the room and down the stairs to Mrs. Chambers' office, but she wasn't there. I hurried to the library and found her talking to Mr. Roth. I stopped short in the doorway, panting.

Mrs. Chambers turned. "Miss Danes, why are you so out of breath?"

"I'm sorry to interrupt. Something's happened."

"Damn, what now?" Mr. Roth said, slamming down the newspaper in his hand.

"The classroom's been vandalized."

Mr. Roth jumped up from his desk chair. "What?"

Mrs. Chambers' hand went to her throat. "Dear me."

"Show us." Mr. Roth led the way.

Somehow, I climbed all those stairs again to the third floor. When I reached the classroom, I held onto the door frame, gasping. They were so upset by the scene they didn't notice my condition, gratefully.

"I should call the police?" Mrs. Chambers asked, visibly stricken.

"Yes, hurry."

She nodded and left the room, shaking her head in disbelief.

"Something serious is definitely going on around here." Mr. Roth stepped carefully away from the clutter. "First the brakes, then this. Did you touch anything?"

"Not a thing. I was too horrified."

"Leave it until the police have dusted for prints."

"Of course." I regained my composure and wondered if I should share my thoughts with him. "Someone is definitely after you. Maybe Ellen? By the words on the blackboard, it could it be me?"

"You? I don't think so. The missing medication, the brakes on my car, the railing along the cliff, and now this. I'm not sure."

"And Ellen's cat."

"What cat? Ellen can't have pets because of her condition."

"I thought so too until she said she lost her cat. Apparently, she had befriended a stray cat and was feeding it."

"Well. What about it?"

"The day I arrived, Ben and I found a cat dead, nailed to a tree."

"Dear God." He raked his fingers through his hair. "Why wasn't I told?"

"I was new. Mrs. Chambers said she'd handle it. And . . . there is the doll I found right before Ellen's party."

"What doll?"

"I've been holding onto it, not sure if it meant anything or not. I should have told someone."

"Tell me now." He spoke with controlled anger. A vein throbbed at his temple.

"It was along the cliff path. One of Ellen's soft plastic dolls. The head's cut off, and stab marks all over its body."

"Is it in your room?"

I nodded.

"Let's go downstairs and wait for the police. We'll pick up the doll on our way."

We left the classroom and just as we reached the top of the stairs, he grabbed my arm, turning me to him.

"Wait, why Ellen? Me, I can understand, but a sweet innocent child?" His brow furrowed. He stared at me as if I had the answer.

I hesitated to speak my mind and chewed on my lip.

"Your expression tells me you have an idea." He let go of my arm.

"Perhaps . . . someone on staff?"

"Impossible."

"How else could someone get in here? Certainly not from the window.

"Then who?" His eyes went wide.

"I hate to suggest this, but I accidentally overhead a strange telephone conversation by Nurse Clayton."

"Nurse Clayton? Why would she want to hurt Ellen?"

"I don't know. It's a terrible thought. She told someone to stop pressuring her, and she knew one thing . . . that you were hiding something. I don't know what she meant. Maybe it isn't about Ellen. It sounds like she's after information about you."

Mr. Roth's face turned white. "How strange. Perhaps you misunderstood her. Hearing a one-sided conversation could get you into trouble."

Why did he look suddenly guilty? Was he hiding something and Sylvi knows? I could not figure that out.

"You're right. Maybe the police should fingerprint all the staff. It would be someone with access."

"That's a good idea. In the meantime, let's not jump to any conclusions about Nurse Clayton. At least, not now."

I agreed.

We went to my room to retrieve the doll I had wrapped in a towel. Mrs. Chambers was sitting on the settee in the parlor. Her fingers nervously tapped her lap. She rose when we entered.

"Oh, Mr. Roth. The police are on their way. I hope they get here soon. This is all so very distressing."

"Calm down, now. Let's all keep our heads." Mr. Roth eyed me directly.

The intercom buzzed. Mr. Roth answered.

"This is Ben, sir. I've let the police in the gate."

Mrs. Chambers opened the door just as the police car pulled up. The same inspector from the car accident entered with two officers. One carried a case. Mr. Roth gave the doll to the inspector, whispering to him. They all proceeded upstairs.

I stayed in the parlor with the housekeeper.

"What does this mean, Miss Danes? All these strange things."

"Not sure. The inspector will figure it out." Wishing I was right, I couldn't help wonder about Sylvi. It made little sense why she would want to hurt Ellen. It must be someone else, but who?

CHAPTER EIGHT

The staff had been buzzing with gossip for days about the vandalism and threats against Mr. Roth and potentially Ellen, although we were instructed not to talk. Who could not? At least I had Mr. Roth to discuss it with, but feigning no knowledge proved difficult.

Though Ellen was still healing, the doctor approved her spending a couple of hours a day on her lessons. I had just left her room and began descending the main staircase, finding Mr. Roth staring at one portrait. I stopped and watched him for a moment.

He looked up with an odd expression. "I didn't realize you were standing there."

"You looked deep in thought."

"I was. Are you on your way to your daily walk?"

"Looking for you, actually. Curious if the police finished fingerprinting the staff? They did mine a couple of days ago."

"All done. Now we wait until the police analyze the prints from the classroom and the brakes of my car. They found prints on the doll, too. They'll compare with everyone on the estate."

"What about the staff who live in town?"

"Them too. Oh, and Mrs. Chambers is having the classroom cleaned up. You'll be able to return in another day."

"Good. I've been worried Ellen would hear about it."

"I've given strict orders. No one is to mention it or talk about it. I don't want her upset."

"I'm glad of that."

Mr. Roth returned his gaze to the portrait.

I stopped to look, too. "All the portraits on this wall are beautifully done."

"They are. I'm studying it. I mean the technique the artist used."

"Why? Who is he?"

"This one is my father, Hugh Roth Senior. Rather dour expression, don't you think?"

"A stern-looking man."

"Unfortunately, he was. Painted maybe forty years ago when he was around my age now. He was forty-three when I came along."

"He was old to have his first born. What about this woman?" I pointed to the portrait a few steps down. A beautiful woman with dark wavy tresses wore a burgundy sequined gown and sequined headband.

"My mother. Beautiful, wasn't she? Even in this painting, she looked sad. Painted in the roaring twenties, judging by all the sequins."

"I can feel her sadness emanating from the painting."

"You are an Empath, Miss Danes."

"I don't know about that."

He crossed his arms and observed me for a few moments, making me nervous, so I changed the subject.

"I've been meaning to ask you something, and I always seem to forget when I'm with you."

"Ask away."

"Where does the name Rothmorton come from?"

"Well . . ." He moved up a few steps. It was the portrait of a stately woman in a lavender-colored dress with leg-of-mutton sleeves. "This was my grandmother, Elizabeth Morton. Her money, combined with my grandfather Howard Roth's, made them both extremely rich. It was shortly after my father was born that they broke ground."

"Oh. I see."

"You guessed it, Rothmorton was born and by the time they completed it, the so-called Gilded Age was in full swing."

"When was this painted?"

"Might have been around 1890. She was maybe late thirties."

"She looks very mature."

"Women in those times aged faster."

"I know the common folk did."

"Common folk." He laughed. "We aren't royalty."

"You know what I mean. My cousin, Orpha, really aged after she turned forty. But she smoked like a chimney."

"You don't smoke."

"Breathing Orpha's smoke was enough. I don't like being around it."

"I sensed you were sensitive to it and why I always ask when you are present."

"Most people don't care, so I appreciate your thoughtfulness. By the way, why are you studying your father's portrait?"

We descended the steps together.

"I'm having my portrait painted. The artist is coming this afternoon to begin."

"That's exciting. I wondered why there wasn't a painting of you on the wall."

"I've resisted as I have with most traditional expectations. The Board of Directors are pressuring me. They want it for the corporate offices. If I like it, the artist will paint a copy for Rothmorton."

We reached the foyer, and the doorbell rang. I nearly jumped out of my skin at the loudness. The only time I'd heard it was at Ellen's party. It was so noisy, I barely heard it. Mr. Roth answered the door, and a man dressed in a gray suit, wearing a hat and carrying a wooden case, greeted him. Ben followed, carrying some equipment.

"Mr. Greene. I'm Hugh Roth." He shook the gentleman's hand and brought him into the foyer.

"Miss Danes, this is Elmer Greene. He is the artist who painted President Hoover."

"What an honor to meet you."

"I'm honored to be here myself." Mr. Greene set down his case and turned his attention to the wall of portraits. "Do you mind if I peruse your gallery first?"

"Not at all." Mr. Roth turned to me.

"I'll leave you to your business. Off to take my walk." I went to the front door.

"If you like, you're welcome to observe later on," Mr. Roth said, "if it's all right with you, Mr. Greene?"

"Absolutely. I'd like to look around. Finding the right light and location is important before I set up my easel," Mr. Greene said.

"Take your time. The parlor is right through there." Mr. Roth pointed.

Mr. Greene wandered off through the parlor and Mr. Roth turned to me again. "I know you're stressed over the vandalism and all the other incidents."

"Yes, I admit it's taken its toll on me, but I'll be okay."

"I have an idea to take our minds off it."

"The portraits?"

"Uh, no. I'd like you to join me tomorrow evening for dinner in Boston." His eyes lit up.

"You mean, like a date?"

"Uh, it could be."

"What about our agreement to keep things professional?" I bit my lip. Why did I bring that up? I was excited at the prospect of going to Boston and being alone with him.

"Well—"

"Besides, how would it look to the rest of the staff?"

"Forget the staff. I know you feel the attraction between us. It's undeniable. Tell me you don't and I'll drop it."

He was right about the attraction, but were we right to indulge ourselves?

"I won't deny there is something there. Your behavior has improved toward me and I am more comfortable with you. But won't there be talk?" My hesitation was not unfounded. I wondered if others were already whispering behind my back.

"It's just dinner . . . and Ben will drive the limo."

My hesitancy was making Mr. Roth nervous. He was shifting from one foot to the other. Knowing Ben would be there made a difference.

"Well, all right. Will it be fancy?"

"Wear your fabulous blue dress. It will be perfect." He took my hand, and I quivered from his gentle touch. I could feel it all the way to my toes and worried I might trip walking out the door. I couldn't help myself. The excitement rose in me, and for the next hour my walk was on air. Glad I had the blue dress, but no dressy coat. Oh well, it's what I had, and it was me. I just hoped I wasn't making a mistake going out with Mr. Roth.

***

The next day was nerve-wracking, filled with anticipation about the evening out. Unsuccessful at remaining focused and calm during Ellen's lessons, my mind wandered. And it wasn't only about the dinner with Mr. Roth. I worried about gossip and if I made a mistake accepting his invitation. I didn't want it to ruin my relationship with him, Ellen, or anyone else at Rothmorton. Hopefully, with Ben driving, he would crush any rumors.

"Miss Danes, why do you keep staring out the window?"

"I'm sorry Ellen, was I?"

"Did I read okay?"

"What? Oh, fine, dear, fine. Keep reading."

Ellen enjoyed reading from the new copies of the Dick and Jane books, but she was already far ahead of their simplistic style.

"Uncle Hugh said he's not coming to dinner tonight."

"He told you?"

"Said you were going with him. Why?"

"Uh, well, he asked me and I'd never been to dinner in Boston. I thought it'd be fun."

"Wish I could go too." Ellen frowned and a twinge of guilt passed over me.

"It would be too late for you by the time we return. Maybe next time."

"Okay." Her face lit up.

"It's almost time for Sylvi to get you. Let's finish up you reading. By the way, did you tell Nurse Clayton about Boston?"

"Uh-huh."

"What did she say?"

"She thought it was nice."

I hadn't had time to tell Sylvi and hoped she wasn't upset with me, considering I told her there was nothing going on between me and Mr. Roth.

***

Mr. Roth told me to be downstairs by half-past five. It was five fifteen, and I wasn't ready. I changed my hairstyle, parting it on the side and wavy to my shoulders, just like Bette Davis wore in a photo I found in an old magazine. I hoped he would notice. My hands shook so much while applying makeup I nearly poked my eye out, applying mascara.

Satisfied by my appearance in the full-length mirror, I made my way down the curved staircase, taking each step carefully, holding onto the rail, just in case.

Mr. Roth stood at the foot of the stairs, dressed in a dark suit and, bless him, he wore a lovely blue and red striped tie. If he were any more handsome, I would have fainted. He held out his hand for mine and we touched, creating the same electric charge my body found enticing.

"You're gorgeous, Dee," he said. "You don't mind I call you Dee, do you?"

"I'm okay with it." A smile involuntarily formed.

"Then call me Hugh, at least when we are alone."

"Okay, and you look pretty good yourself, Hugh." I smiled so broadly, my mouth hurt, but I couldn't help it.

Hugh nodded to someone in the shadows of the staircase. Mrs. Chambers came forward holding out a fur coat.

"This should fit you perfectly." Hugh took it from Mrs. Chambers.

"I shouldn't. It's too much." I took a step back.

"Consider it a loan for the evening. It might be a little outdated. It was my mother's."

"We had it taken out of storage. The furriers cleaned and delivered it today just for tonight, Miss Danes," Mrs. Chambers said. "Go ahead, put it on." She seemed pleased.

I took a cautious step forward and Hugh helped me into the dark brown mink cape, reaching just below my waist. There were slits for my arms and the collar stood up against my neck.

"It feels marvelous. I've never even touched mink before. So soft." My hands caressed the front of the cape as I fumbled with the closure. He helped, while smiling ear to ear.

"You two make a lovely couple. Have a good time." Mrs. Chambers waved as we went out and down the front steps.

Ben was standing with the limousine door open. Hugh held my hand as I slipped into the back seat, making sure my full skirt was inside before Ben shut the door. Hugh ran around to the other side, sliding next to me, very close. Ben took the limo slow around the fountain and down the drive.

I had not thought about Jane Eyre in ages. Mr. Rochester would not have taken Jane on a date. I chuckled half out loud.

"What's so funny?"

"Nothing. I'm delirious with wonder. By the way, where's the other seat that Ellen sat in when we went to your yacht?"

"That's temporary for extra seating when needed."

"There's so much more room now."

"Hmmm. You know. You look just like Bette Davis with your hair fixed like that."

"I do?" I pretended to be surprised and happiness filled me.

He took my hand gently in his. I was on cloud ten and a half. "Would you like a glass of champagne?" He pushed a button and a door in the car's side slowly lowered, revealing a mini-bar with champagne glasses and a bucket of ice bearing a bottle.

"That's a surprise." I said. "Didn't notice the last time."

"The bar is always there. We just didn't need it. Only for special occasions."

He popped the cork and poured two round stem glasses. He touched his glass to mine and the chime of the crystal rang out. "Here's to our first . . . may I say it . . . date."

"Is this a date?"

"What do you think?"

"I think it's mah-velous, dah-ling." We both laughed at my imitation.

Before I knew it, we were in Boston, and the sun was almost set. The traffic slowed us down. I peered out the windows at my first view of Boston at night. We drove into the downtown area and passed some of the original buildings from our country's early beginnings, wedged between tall buildings. It looked so strange to me.

"Oh, I'd love to do the historic walk sometime, Hugh."

"I love it when you call me Hugh." He nudged my shoulder, tilting his head toward me. "We should plan to do it with Ellen."

"She would love it. I've been teaching her a little about American History since we live in such a historic locale."

"Great."

"We're here, Mr. Roth," Ben said through the window.

Hugh took my empty glass and put them away. He and Ben got out of the limo. They stopped and talked for a minute or two. Their heads huddled together as if they were conferring over something important. Hugh's face looked worried, and I wondered what was going on.

Hugh opened my door, and I stumbled, even with him holding my hand.

"Whoops. Sorry. Too much champagne," I giggled. "What were you talking about with Ben?"

"Oh nothing. Let's go inside. I'm starving."

Something told me he was lying. I didn't want to spoil the evening by worrying, so I didn't press. The name of the restaurant was lit up in neon across the top of the building and couples dressed to the hilt were ahead of us wearing their elegant furs. My fingers ran along my mink's collar, giving me a sense of importance. I reveled in the moment.

Hugh checked the fur and his overcoat with the hat-check girl, and the maître d' ushered us to a secluded corner booth. An orchestra played "Blue

Moon," my favorite song, to couples dancing on a large parquet-wood dance floor. Hugh ordered champagne—as if I hadn't had enough already. I burped and flamed bright red, but he didn't notice.

"I know exactly what we should have. Do you mind if I order for you?"

"Not at all." Entranced at his self-assurance for I wouldn't have known what to order since the menu was in a foreign language. While I swayed with the music, Hugh rattled off our order in French as if it were his native tongue. When the waiter left, Hugh offered his hand.

"Care to dance?"

"I'd love to, but I'm afraid I'm not very good."

"Let me be the judge."

He led me through the tables and to the dance floor when the tune switched to "Moonlight Serenade."

"I love this tune," I said, putting my hand on his shoulder.

He took my other hand and swung me around in a circle. I could have swooned.

"It's an oldie, but goodie. Hey, you dance just fine."

With his cheek against mine, the warmth of his hand at the curve of my back holding me close, my body molded together with his. We swayed and moved to the music as if we were Fred Astaire and Ginger Rogers.

"You smell divine," he whispered in my ear, his lips lighting against my skin.

"So do you," I whispered back as his grip tightened, twirling me around and around till I was dizzy with the dancing, the champagne, and him. I closed my eyes without a care, letting the world pass us by.

"We should go back. The champagne is waiting," he said, drawing me reluctantly to our corner.

"I'm having such a wonderful time."

He gave me a radiant smile. "I am too. Don't worry, it wasn't our last dance, you know."

The food came in courses and Hugh explained what everything was: escargot, vichyssoise, coq au vin, and crème brûlée for dessert. I thought I might burst and welcomed more dancing.

Hugh twirled me around on the floor.

"I've never danced like this before. Are you a magician?"

"Maybe, or you didn't have the right partners." He leaned his head over my shoulder, his breath warm and inviting.

"I don't want this night to end."

"Me neither." His lips brushed against my cheek, sending tingling ripples down my arms.

We were the last ones on the dance floor. The orchestra conductor said, "Goodnight and come back soon," and they played the last notes.

I leaned into Hugh's shoulder as he guided me off the dance floor. I grabbed my clutch, and he retrieved his coat and my fur, and we strolled out of the restaurant to wait for Ben.

He arrived late and was a bit disheveled. Hugh gave him a stern look. I didn't want to be Ben right then. So, I slipped into the back seat, but Hugh shut the door, leaving me alone. He and Ben once again huddled together over something. Ben handed a piece of paper to Hugh and, by his reaction, it wasn't good.

Hugh got in the car and Ben drove the limo out of town. I waited impatiently for an explanation.

"He had a flat tire."

"Is that all? Then why do you look so distraught?"

He exhaled and stretched out his arms as if readying himself. "I didn't want to ruin our dinner, but when we arrived, Ben told me he thought someone had been following us. When he parked the limo, he had left it briefly to uh . . . freshen up, you know, and when he returned, he found a knife stuck in a tire."

"A knife!" I gripped his arm and leaned into him. Even with the fur cape, I shivered from fear and worry. It was all too much. "I'm scared."

"I know. Sorry. I'll sort this out, I promise." He tensed.

"Is there something else?"

He sighed. "There was a note on the windshield." He took a piece of paper from his pocket and handed it to me.

When I opened it, the words made me sick to my stomach. In the same uneven scrawl as on the blackboard:

"Oh, my God. Should you call the police here in Boston before we leave?"

"Ben did and made a statement. The police asked around the immediate area if anyone saw someone near the limo. Nothing. That's why Ben was late. I'll call the inspector on the case in Plymouth when I get home."

"What about the note?"

"The inspector will want to compare it against the handwriting from the chalkboard. He took photos."

"What does the note mean? Get away with what?"

"I don't know." His face was tense with worry.

It was a quiet ride back to Rothmorton. Snuggling up to Hugh with his arms around me made me feel safe for the moment.

Hugh called the police inspector when we arrived at the mansion. The inspector would come by the next morning. He walked me up the stairs to my room. After everything had happened, I was awkward and unsure what might happen. We stopped at my door and I turned to him.

"Despite the horrible ending, it was a wonderful first date." I gazed at his worried face. Maybe he thought the whole evening was a wash-up. His hands went under the fur and around my waist, pulling me toward him. I shuddered at his touch, wanting so much to press my lips to his.

He stopped. "Something changed at dinner, didn't it?"

"Yes, it did."

"You must know how incredibly attracted I am to you. It's not just that. I find you intelligent and interesting, too." He sounded like a schoolboy talking to a girl for the first time.

"That's nice to hear. And . . . I'm attracted to you." I couldn't believe I was encouraging him, but everything had changed and I no longer wanted to hold back.

"Really?" His face lit up and butterflies filled my stomach. He leaned in closer. "May I?"

"Yes." My voice, a mere whisper.

When his lips pressed against mine, my body came alive as if he had flicked a switch, sending titillating sensations all over my body. Something I'd not experienced with any of the boys in college. Hugh was a man, not a boy. He knew what he wanted, and he wanted to kiss me, and boy, did he. I melted into a buttery mess as my hands followed an involuntary impulse moving up his chest and around his neck. My fingers curled into his thick, wavy hair and we both moaned.

It took all my strength to open the door and go inside.

"Good night, Dee," he said, leaning his hand against the doorjamb.

I touched my lips and smiled, dumbstruck. Or was it love struck?

Softly closing the door, I listened to his footsteps disappear down the hall. I turned on the light and twirled around in the center of the room. Like a silly schoolgirl after her first school dance. Giddy with happiness, I went to the full-length mirror and gazed at my reflection. Why had I been so resistant? He's not what I originally thought. He's wonderful, and I loved how I felt when I was with him. Something inside me stirred. Desire.

CHAPTER NINE

The next morning, the inspector picked up the note and took our statements. I didn't have much to say since I witnessed nothing. They put an extra detail on Ellen, a policewoman in plain clothes. We expected her to arrive in the afternoon to meet Ellen, Sylvi, and me.

"She'll just be an extra person surrounding Ellen for her protection," Hugh told me in private. "The policewoman and any change of guard would sit outside Ellen's bedroom at night. You should feel extra safe, too."

"I'm worried how this will affect Ellen."

"Me too. We need to make light of it. I don't want her afraid."

"How will you explain the guard outside her room?"

"She won't know, unless, God forbid, something should happen. The guard will leave when Sylvi goes to Ellen's room to check on her in the morning."

"Makes sense. If Ellen needs Sylvi, the adjoining door between their rooms would keep Ellen from walking into the hallway. Though she doesn't usually, anyway."

"It will be fine." He leaned in, staring at my lips like he wanted to kiss me. I wanted to kiss him. During the day, anyone could pop into the library. With great restraint, we parted.

The next day, Hugh held a meeting in the staff dining area. Everyone chattered what could it was about.

"Your attention, please. I need to emphasize this is serious." He waited until they all quieted down. "There have been several disturbing incidents, as you already know, against me and possibly aimed at Ellen. We have increased security staff on the estate. I want everyone here to understand the importance of sticking to the house rules of no overnight guests.

"Family and friends must be authorized for access to the grounds until further notice. Also, no one is to mention these goings on with Ellen. It's grounds for dismissal. I don't want her living in fear."

Hugh was stern, and the staff gave concerned looks at him and each other. Mumbling their agreement, they whispered among themselves as they left the area.

Sylvi wasn't there, she was with Ellen, keeping her occupied. Mrs. Chambers stayed behind with me and Hugh.

"Dear Lordy, Mr. Roth," Mrs. Chamber said. "It's a terrible situation, but I'm glad you made this announcement, so there's no misunderstanding. Is there anything you need from me?"

"Not right now, Mrs. Chambers. Thank you." Hugh glanced at me briefly, signaling with his eyes upward, then left.

I nodded my head, assuming he meant for me to meet him upstairs in the library. After a few minutes chatting with Mrs. Chambers, I excused myself. He stood at the open French doors, smoking a cigarette.

"Any news from the inspector?"

"Not yet, I was—"

The library door swung open and in stormed Sylvi, her eyes flashing and her mouth twisted strangely.

"Where is she?" Sylvi screamed at Hugh.

"I beg your pardon," he said.

"Where did you take her? She's gone."

"I don't know what you mean. Who's gone?"

"Your wife . . . and my sister."

Hugh closed the French Door and doused his cigarette in an ashtray on his desk. "What are you talking about?" He and shot a glance my way.

I'm sure my face told him exactly what I was feeling. "You're sister?" I directed at Sylvi, confused by her claim.

Sylvi whipped around and raised her hand with her finger pointing at me. "And you! I'm sorry, Dee, but what kind of person are you to get involved with a married man?" She sneered a vicious face.

"I never!" My stomach turned somersaults, and I thought I might vomit. The dramatic change in Sylvi gave me pause, and I took a step back. "He's not married."

"He's been telling people he's not, but he's still married to my sister. There was no annulment." Sylvi stood with her hands on her hips.

"Is this true?" I turned to Mr. Roth.

Ignoring my question, kept his eyes on Sylvi. "Your accusations are baseless, and besides, my wife didn't have a sister. She would have told me."

"I can prove she's my sister. Why she didn't mention me is strange."

"Well, she didn't."

I backed away from the two of them. If what Sylvi said was true, I had no business being in the room. Hugh saw me inching towards the door and flashed his eyes and shook his head slightly. He wanted me to stay.

Sylvi went to the window talking absently. "We were at odds when she joined the service, but it wasn't me who kept us apart. Nora was the one to hold grudges, not me. I loved her."

"Wait a minute, have you ever gone by the name of Sly?" Hugh stepped toward her.

Sylvi turned to him. Her hand went to her throat, and her eyes teared. "Nora was the only person who called me Sly. How do you know the name if you didn't know about me?"

"I found an unfinished letter addressed to a Sly. Thought it was a friend she hadn't mentioned. Didn't think anything of it. If you're Nora's sister, why take so long to find her? It's been years. And . . . why the deception at becoming Ellen's nurse?"

Why didn't he deny there wasn't an annulment? They were talking as if he were still married. It's Jane Eyre all over again. It couldn't really be happening to me. I clutched my stomach in agony.

"I don't understand." My voice, a mere whisper. I took the nearest chair and stared at the two of them. They'd forgotten I was in the room.

Sylvi paced the room, wringing her hands. "I'm Nora's younger sister. She joined the Navy Nurse Corps during the war. I didn't enlist until '44, just before they stopped recruiting nurses. I'd lost contact with Nora. Didn't know what happened to her until the Navy notified me she was missing.

"Right before the war ended, I received a letter from Nora. They had rescued her from a POW camp and she was working at a hospital in California. She briefly mentioned a patient she had fallen in love with. That was in '45."

Hugh nodded his head. "The year I met her. I was a patient at the Naval Hospital in San Francisco."

"Yes. I kept writing, but my letters were returned as undeliverable with no forwarding address. The Navy didn't have an address either."

"Where were you stationed?" Hugh leaned against his desk.

"In Europe. It wasn't until three years ago, a letter forwarded from my APO address was from Nora, postmarked 1946." Sylvi threw her hands in the air and plopped into the chair next to me.

She didn't look at me, or she would have seen my distress.

"You got a letter four years later?" Hugh's brows drew together. "Unbelievable."

"Crazy, I know," Sylvi said. "She wrote she was getting married and moving to Massachusetts."

He rubbed his eyes, then dragged his hands down his face. "But that was three years ago?"

"It wasn't until a few months ago I figured out where in Massachusetts she meant. I sent letters to the hospital in San Francisco searching for nurses who had worked with Nora. I'd hoped to find out where she went and with whom.

"Finally, a nurse who worked with her wrote to me. She thought the man's name was Drew or Hugh. She didn't know where they went. The Navy looked up patients with those names and sent me a list. I started in Boston. This was a year ago. When I ran across something about you in the newspaper at Rothmorton Insurance, I tried to reach you. But whenever I called, your office said you were working from home. I came here asking for Mr. and Mrs. Hugh Roth."

"And what were you told?" His head popped up at that.

"That the Mrs. moved away, and you weren't home. They asked me if I was here for the nursing job. I said yes. When Mrs. Chambers hired me, I thought it was a sign. I was desperate to find out what happened to Nora."

"Why didn't you just ask me?"

"Because of the warning when I accepted the job. You know . . . about never mentioning your wife or talking about her. I knew something wasn't right, so I investigated, secretly."

"What makes you think I've done something to her?"

I looked up at him, trying to read his face. It told me nothing, and I didn't know what to think about Sylvi's story. All the lies and deception made my head spin. I thought Sylvi was my friend.

"I found this?" Sylvi thrust out a piece of paper. "Proof Nora was a patient at the Asylum in White Hill, for psychiatric care, admitted in '46. And . . . the bills were paid until '47 . . . by you."

"Where did you get it?" Mr. Roth grabbed it from her hand.

"From your files, where else?"

"You broke into my desk and papers while under my employment?" He glared at Sylvi. "It was my father, Hugh Roth Sr., who paid those bills."

His anger made me cringe, although he had reason. Apparently, so did Sylvi. I couldn't make sense of the conversation. He committed his wife to a psychiatric asylum?

Sylvi continued, "Oh, that makes sense. But with all the secrecy, how else would I get the truth? I went to find her. The asylum said she wasn't a patient. Even when I showed them the form, and told them I was her sister, they denied she was ever there. So, where did you send her and why are none of your employees allowed to speak of Nora? What are you hiding?"

"It's been you all this time?" I blurted, unable to hold my tongue a moment more. "You killed Ellen's cat. You left the adrenaline behind. You cut the brakes on Mr. Roth's car. You vandalized the classroom. It must have been you who slashed the limo's tires and left the threatening note while we were in Boston. You knew about the trip to Boston!"

"No! I would never hurt Ellen or Mr. Roth. It's not why I'm here," Sylvi said.

"I can't hear any more of this." I covered my ears with my hands and ran out of the room.

"Miss Danes, Dee." Hugh said.

Throwing clothes into my bag, my hands trembled with anger and disgust. My fingers fumbled with the latch on the suitcase. Gazing around the room, a lump formed in my throat. I needed space from the lies and deceit. Down the back stairs and past Mrs. Chambers' office, I heard her call to me. Ignoring her, I rushed out the door and down the steps, across the courtyard toward Ben, working on the roadster.

I half expected Mr. Roth to come after me, but he didn't.

"Ben, take me to town. Now!"

"Now?" He looked at my suitcase, perplexed.

"The green car, right?"

Before he could open the back door, I slipped into the front seat. Ben put my suitcase in the backseat, then drove the car out of the courtyard and through the circular drive. I turned around just as Hugh was coming out the front door, waving and yelling.

"Stop! Come back."

"Don't stop the car, Ben. Please keep going." My heart was beating wildly.

He did as I bade and I brushed away the tears streaming down my cheeks. We rode in uncomfortable silence. Ben kept glancing my way, probably hoping I would say something. My mind swirled with Sylvi's words. Hugh had a wife hidden in an asylum? Who was this man? Did I ever really know him? Or had he shown me the man he wanted me to know? It was all too much for me. I wanted to scream at the top of my lungs. I thought of Jane Eyre? Did she feel what I did? Wait, she was a character in a book. This was my life, and real, and they shattered it to pieces. I clutched my hands so tightly my knuckles turned white.

"We're almost to town. Where do you want me to take you?" Ben said in a gentle tone.

"A hotel. Any is fine." I dared not look at him directly for fear I would come unglued. My body was like a rubber band stretched so tight it might pop, and all my emotions would explode. I didn't want him to see.

He turned off the main highway and headed toward the coast. A sign on the side of the road with an arrow said: Windsor House Inn, with a private beach.

Perfect, out of the way of the main drag. I didn't want anyone to find me. Ben stopped in front of a two-story building with a narrow columned entrance.

"Promise me you won't tell anyone where you took me. I need some time alone. Do you understand?"

"Uh, sure thing, Miss Danes. Let me get your bag."

He went around the car and opened my door for me as I sat immobile and rigid. He held out his hand, and I took it. Stumbling out of the vehicle, he steadied me with his grip. "Thanks, Ben. I'm a bit wobbly."

"You sure you're alright?"

"I'll be fine. I've had a shock, is all."

"How long are you going to stay here?"

"Not sure. I might go home to the farm." In my heart, it was no longer my home.

"Go back to Illinois?" He cocked his head.

"Perhaps."

"Hey, Miss Danes, if you need anything, anything at all, just call me."

"I doubt I'll be calling the estate."

"Can I come and check on you? To make sure you're alright."

He was genuinely concerned, and it was comforting.

"Give me a couple of days and call me here."

"I will." He gave me a sincere smile and followed me inside, setting my bag at the registration desk.

The man behind the desk gave me a pleasant smile and nodded to Ben. "How are you doing, Ben?"

"Good," Ben said with a strange sheepish grin, and left.

"Friend of yours?" I said to the clerk.

"Uh, I see him around, ya know, small town. How may I help you?"

I took a single room. Not sure what I would do. I wondered about Ben, whether he brought his adoring women here. I took the room key from the desk clerk. He directed me to the stairway to the second floor. He offered to have someone take up my bag, but I refused and picked up the bag myself. I wanted to be alone and as soon as possible.

I was numb with shock, dismay, and possibly a broken heart. How could Hugh lie to me?

CHAPTER TEN

The room was clean and quaint, with ruffled curtains on the narrow windows letting in soft light. My body sank into an easy chair. Tears threatened, but I held them back. The whole situation was impossible, and just like Jane, I ran away the moment I learned he was still married. What a horrid twist of fate Hugh's wife was asylum material. Of course, I didn't know why Mrs. Roth was in the asylum. What was her name, Nora? I had thought his wife was out of the picture.

My disgust over the lies overshadowed what Sylvi had said about her sister. I recalled her mentioning her sister had been a prisoner of war. Her experiences could have been related to her mental state. I didn't want to imagine what happened to her.

The rule not to talk about Hugh's wife was a lie. It made little sense. I had assumed he was so broken up about the failed marriage. What was he was afraid of . . . a scandal? An important secret to keep. He was still a married man.

My chest hurt so much. Most of the romance novels I read were about broken hearts. I couldn't imagine what the pain was actually like. It was horrendous that Hugh could break my heart. A revelation that made me even more sad. I had just admitted to my attraction to him. Now I learn it runs much deeper, and he is unavailable. A sob welled up from deep within me, slowly moving upward till it burst forth from my mouth into an agonizing sound. I grabbed the pillow from the bed to muffle my voice.

Tears drenched the pillowcase. I moved to the bed, rolling onto my side, one hand on my stomach still roiling almost to the point of retching. When the sobbing stopped, I stared at the ceiling, watching the flicker of light coming through the window curtains.

I questioned what kind of man maintains such lies for years. My head and my heart throbbed with pain at losing someone I didn't quite have.

Needing to clear my head, I left the room. Paths led down to a private beach. The salt air calmed me as I rolled up the legs of my pants to my knees and removed my shoes to dangle from one hand. The wet sand seeped up between my toes as I stepped toward the slow-moving waves, allowing the brisk water to splash against my ankles. People swam in the ocean, though the swimming season had passed. The wind whipped around me as an older couple walked by. Perhaps they were on vacation or retired and enjoying life. Their faces smiling at each other with love. My heart tugged again and a sob deep within threatened.

The beach was long. I could barely see the roof of the Inn. Tired and dejected, I stared out at the sea and its rolling waves. Sea shells peaked just above the sand and I picked up several, cleaning them in the salt water. I had been at Rothmorton for weeks without walking on a beach, so engrossed in my life with Ellen and Hugh.

"Dee!"

The sun was directly at me, though I shaded my eyes with my hand. I knew who it was striding toward me with his long legs stomping on the stand, still wearing his shoes. He stopped ten feet away. I took a step back.

"Don't," Hugh said. "Just hear me out. Please. You don't know everything. Let me tell you."

I wanted to hear more. I needed an explanation to make sense of everything.

"Can we walk together?" He held out his hand.

I nodded, ignoring the outstretched hand, and we strolled back toward the Inn. "Ben told you where I was. Didn't he?"

"No. I had called all the hotels by the time he returned to the estate. Please listen to me."

"Nothing you say could change how I feel. You are married. I've wondered why you didn't allow the staff to mention her name. It was odd, but I figured she hurt you. But it's all lies, isn't it?"

"Yes, lies, but it's not what you think. It's worse—but let me explain. Maybe, just maybe, you might understand a little."

I turned away, not wanting to hear anything that was worse than what I had already heard. Hugh made a sound of defeat and I looked back at him. He clenched his hands, his eyes red. Had he been crying? My heart lunged for him. I waited to hear more. "I'm listening."

He took a deep breath. "Let me start at the beginning. I was in the war, like others, and injured. Nora was my nurse. It was 1945, right before the war ended. The entire world was crazy. We barely knew each other, but we fell in love and got married as soon as they released me and discharged from service. We came straight to Rothmorton, since neither of us had anywhere else to go. But, my father..." He stopped and shoved his hands deep into his pockets, then let out a long sigh.

"My father hit the roof. He wanted me to get an annulment right away, but I refused. I was adamant about it . . . and should have been about other things. Maybe it would have been different. When it came to my father, I was a sniveling weakling. He used that to manipulate me." He picked up a shell, turning it over and over in his hands. His eyes looked so far away. He must have been thinking about Nora.

I said nothing, waiting.

"Father finally backed down and Nora and I stayed, but she was having trouble sleeping, terrible nightmares, and fell into a deep depression. She wouldn't talk about it. My father insisted she see a doctor, and she agreed, a couple of them. Pills helped her sleep, but the nightmares continued to plague her . . . waking screaming. She tried to commit suicide . . ."

I gasped. My hand reached out and touched his arm. He gave me a haunted look filled with so much pain.

"There was only one thing to do," he continued. "We took her to a private hospital for treatment. Father wanted it kept secret. That's when the lies started. He made me tell people she went home to visit relatives. He wanted me to leave, to avoid questions. I refused. When she was there three months, they discovered she was pregnant."

"Pregnant?" The word burst from my lips.

He stared out at the vast ocean. "I knew it wasn't mine."

"How?" It was unimaginable.

"She wouldn't tell anyone, her doctors, or me, who it was, or how it happened. The facility prided itself on its security. Ha! They were adamant it wasn't a staff member.

"I went nuts trying to come to grips with it. I was angry, wanting to know who was responsible. She held it all inside, and it only made her depression worse. I imagined various scenarios. Was it rape? Consensual? Either was horrible. It tore me apart. My love for her couldn't help and it hurt terribly. To make matters worse, I worried what my father would do when the baby was born."

I found my voice. "What happened when the child came?"

"The child was born in August 1947. It was a difficult birth, hours of labor and then the inconceivable happened . . . Nora died."

"My God. She died?"

"Eclampsia. It devastated me."

"I don't understand. The rumors. Mrs. Chambers told . . ." My mind went into a tailspin and I needed to sit down. I looked around, spotting a wooden stairway from the beach to a walkway. Hugh followed me and we sat on the steps, side by side. I stared out at the ocean while he talked.

He rested his elbows on his knees, hands shaking. "There's more."

"I'm still listening."

"My father took control of the whole situation. I can't explain to you what kind of hold he had on people, especially me. He was a dynamic and manipulative person. Everyone around him would bow to his desires and demands, including me."

"What did he do?"

"He paid everyone off to hide the death and deny she was ever there, and they sealed the records."

"But why?"

He laughed almost hysterically. "Why else? Father couldn't stand for a scandal. Remember, he didn't want me married to her, anyway. He didn't want people to know my wife was pregnant. Especially by another man. Even nationally, it would have been a big deal. Our family was well known. I told my father I would say it was mine, legally the child was mine, since Nora gave birth while we were married. He wouldn't have it and didn't want the child here. It made more sense to him to lie about her death than risk the truth coming out. He sent the child away to be raised by a family in Pennsylvania. Or so he told me." He threw the shell into the ocean with force.

"I don't understand. What about the annulment story?"

"Rumors he spread so people wouldn't wonder what happened between us, or where she went. And as luck would have it, no one really cared. Nora wasn't here long. She had made no friends before being admitted."

"I see. What did you do?"

"I left Rothmorton. Traveled to South America and the Caribbean. I didn't want to lie. A year later, I heard my father was very sick. By the time I returned home, he had died."

"You must have been devastated, so soon after . . ." I reached out to him and touched his hand. His fingers circled mine.

"Relieved, actually. As the heir, everything came to me. I took over the business. For a year, I searched . . . and found the child, and brought her here. Not knowing how to deal with the truth, I told more lies. About who Ellen is. But she is Nora's daughter, the only thing I had left of her."

"Ellen is Nora's daughter?" That piece of information went down like coarse salt.

He turned to me. "So now you know the whole truth."

The sound of the wind and the ocean roared around us. We sat motionless, my hand in his.

"Where is Sylvi? Did you tell her this, too?"

He drew a deep breath. "I told her. She was angrier than before because she wasn't told her sister had died. I thought she'd kill me. She's grieving now, after the fact. If I'd known about her, maybe things would have been different. I don't know. My father and I didn't think Nora had any family."

"It's quite a story. I feel awful about Sylvi. All the lies and deception hiding these secrets are difficult for me to handle."

Hugh's hands had wrapped around both of mine. He stared into my eyes. Looking for forgiveness, perhaps?

"I can understand why she did it. Hell, I've been living a lie for years. Sylvi loves Ellen, and being her aunt was something she hadn't counted on. She's staying at Rothmorton and bringing her husband here so she can be close to Ellen."

"Wait, Sylvi is married? Another secret to add to the pile. Must have been her husband, I heard her talking to. I thought she was the one causing all the trouble around here."

"Well, it's not her, I'm sure of it. And the problem is still hanging over our heads."

"Yes, it is. What happens now with Sylvi knowing the truth? Are you going to tell Ellen?"

"Good God, no! Ellen is too young to understand the whole story. We both agreed Ellen should know Sylvi is her aunt, but I don't think she's ready to know her mother was my wife. Eventually, she will need to know. I'm not sure how to handle the truth about Nora."

"It needs to be dealt with." I gently released my hands from his and those protective walls surrounded me. It was too much to grasp.

He stared at my hands as I returned them to my lap. "I know. At least it wasn't Sylvi causing the vandalism and cutting the brakes."

"Are you sure?"

"I heard from the inspector. He cleared the staff from the fingerprinting."

"This means whoever did all those things . . ."

"Is still out there."

I shivered at the thought.

"Will you come back with me?" His eyes pleaded for me to agree.

"There is so much to process. I-I have feelings for you all jumbled up with what's happened today. I need time to process. The lies and deception on your part and Sylvi's is overwhelming."

"I understand, Dee. Sorry you got caught up in it. You must know how happy it makes me to hear you have feelings for me. I have feelings for you too. Because of you, feelings I thought were dead have surfaced. Please come back with me."

"I don't know. I need to call my cousin, Orpha. Before everything happened this morning, I received a note from Daisy, Orpha's best friend, asking me to call. It's long distance and Orpha is a penny pincher, you know."

"How about tomorrow? I'll call to see where you stand?"

"You may call." My convoluted emotions churned within me. I wanted to be alone and think.

He reached for my hand, but I withdrew. Touching him would only confuse me more. We walked back to the Inn and when he drove away, my heart raced. Despite the feelings we both admitted, Hugh had a lot to face. I didn't want to be in the middle of it.

CHAPTER ELEVEN

When the phone rang, I stopped packing and answered. "I was just about to call you. Orpha is sick."

"Is it serious?"

"She won't tell me. I need to go there. You understand, don't you? I'm not running away. I'll be back."

"You better be back. I need you. Ellen needs you."

"Good to know. I'll miss everyone . . .." My hesitation was clear to me. I needed the time away to figure out what was important to me, not him, not Ellen.

"How long?"

"Not sure. I'll call once I get there."

"Reverse the charges."

"Okay. Oh, and Mr. Roth—"

"It's Hugh, remember?"

"Hugh . . . tell Ellen I'm sorry I didn't say goodbye in person. I'll make it up to her."

"I will. She asked about you last night. I said you had a headache."

"Thank you. Tell Sylvi . . . When I return, I'll talk to her. I just can't right now."

"I'm sure she'll understand."

"Thanks. I'll call soon."

When I hung up, my stomach twisted something fierce. I hated leaving Ellen since she had just come home from the hospital. I would miss Hugh, too, but with reservations. The worry about Orpha was strong. She was all the family I had left. Despite our disagreements, I cared for her in a disconnected way.

When I checked out of the Inn, Hugh had paid my bill and left me an envelope filled with cash for my trip. Ben was waiting outside the hotel to take me to the train station in Boston. I sat up front again.

"You gonna tell me what's going on?" Ben asked.

"I'm going home for a visit and I'll be back. My cousin is sick."

"Sorry, but I'm glad you're comin' back." He grinned.

"How do you know Mr. Roth? You mentioned once the job was a favor."

"Mr. Roth and me were in the war together. I was this runt kid who didn't know nothin' and he kinda took me under his wing. I was scared silly when he got hit."

"You took shrapnel in your leg?"

"Yep. He told me when I was out to look him up. When I did, he gave me this job. He knew I loved cars. In the service, I worked on jeeps and stuff. He's the best."

"He is, isn't he?"

"You sweet on him, aren't ya'? I see how you look at him."

I sent him a shocked look. "Don't make up things that aren't true, Ben." I wasn't ready to acknowledge my feelings for Hugh with anyone until I was sure. And I wasn't sure.

Ben shrugged his shoulders and chuckled. "Yeah, sure thing."

He left me at the train station, making me promise to notify him when my train got into Boston upon my return.

***

The train ride home seemed longer going back than when I had left. My emotions were topsy-turvy, what with everything going on at Rothmorton and my apprehension at seeing Orpha. Sleeping on the train didn't come easy, even though Hugh had purchased a private berth for me. His generosity overflowed to ensure my return. It had a positive effect on me, I couldn't deny. I needed a clear head to deal with Orpha and my body ached when I showed up at her house via taxi, just before dusk. I still had my key, but knocked, not wanting to startle her.

"Deirdre?" Daisy opened the door. "Well, bless your heart. Come on in. I thought you would call me to pick you up at the bus depot." She was about Orpha's age, but looked fifteen years younger. Her blonde hair, styled in a short bob, framed her heart-shaped face.

"I didn't want to bother you. Is Orpha worse?" I put down my things and gave her a hug. "I wasn't expecting to find you here."

The house smelled of mold and dust, and the familiar negative energy still pervaded the place I lived for seven years of my life. Nothing I did could ever change it, because of Orpha's general mood and attitude. The tiny living room was tidy, probably Daisy's doing, if Orpha wasn't well.

"She stays in bed most of the time. I check on her every day. You go on in. She might be sleeping. I'll finish up and air this place out." She rolled her eyes and pinched her nose, leaving the front door open with the screen shut.

When I entered Orpha's room, her eyes were closed. The emotions I thought were behind me came flooding back. She lay in a double bed covered with a multi-colored crocheted afghan. Gingham curtains on the windows and a rocking chair in the corner next to the bed. The room hadn't changed, cluttered with bric-à-brac passed down from her family. She was the last of her family line and I of mine. It brought an unexpected sadness beyond the usual tension. I stood at the foot of her bed, watching her ragged breathing.

She opened her faded blue eyes and blinked at me. "Dee Dee? My goodness gracious girl. Let me look at you. You look terrible." Her voice was weak, but just as cantankerous.

"It was a long train ride." I sat in the rocker. "I'm worried about you. You don't look so good yourself."

Orpha's once chestnut hair had turned gray with patches of white, and cut short.

"Worried? Since when?" She coughed and gagged into a handkerchief, rolling it up and hiding under her covers.

"Since always, Orpha. Why must you question everything I say?" The frustration already mounted. I clenched my teeth and reminded myself she was sick.

"Oh, I don't know." Orpha sighed with resignation. "You bring out that side of me, I suppose."

"Me and everyone else around you. I didn't come back to argue. Have you seen a doctor?"

"That quack, Dr. Brown? Yes."

"And what did he say?"

"Something in my lungs. Makes me weak as all get out."

"What's in your lungs?"

Orpha turned her face away from me and grimaced, putting the hanky to her mouth and coughed again. I could see bloody spittle in the hanky. I shuddered with shock.

"Well?"

"It's cancer," said Daisy, standing at the doorway. "She won't say it. I don't blame her. It's all the smoking."

"Dear God. I'm so sorry Orpha." I reached out to her, but she turned on her side.

"You don't need to be here to watch me wither away. Just go back to your fancy job with the rich folk."

"I'm here and I'm going to stay. Whatever you need. Let me help."

Daisy sat on the opposite side of the bed. "Now, Orpha, you have the two of us to care for you. Are you going to let us? Or do we need to pack you off to a nursing home?"

Daisy had spunk and Orpha let her get away with it. Not me. If I spoke to her that way, we'd end up in a huge argument, me storming out the door, or out of state.

"Please don't send me away. I can't fight the both of you." Orpha rolled onto her back and coughed again.

Daisy and I wouldn't have sent her away, but Orpha responded well to threats.

The next day, I called the doctor for details. Orpha had little time left. He said it could be weeks or days. By the time she saw him, her condition was in the advanced stage. It was right before I had left two months ago. She refused surgery. Though the doctor told me it wouldn't extend her life by much.

I spent the next week caring for Orpha, cooking, cleaning, helping her with her baths. And she fought against my help as much as she was able. Her physical weakness worked in my favor. By the end of the night, I'd fall on my old bed.

It was strange being in my room. The simple furnishings. Nothing had moved. It was as if it was waiting for me. Even if Orpha wasn't dying, I wouldn't be able to return to my former life. I could sense the pull of Rothmorton. "Darn." I had left my copy of *Jane Eyre* behind. Another parallel between my life and Jane's was she returned to her dying aunt. I returned to my dying cousin. Unlike Jane, I wanted to care for Orpha in her last days.

***

"Operator, I'd like to make a collect call, please." I gave the number and waited for the line to connect.

"Rothmorton Estates, Mrs. Chambers speaking."

"Collect call for anyone from a Dee Danes. Will you accept charges?" the Operator said.

"Yes, of course. Miss Danes. Just a minute." There were muffled voices in the background.

"Mr. Roth is picking up the extension." I waited only moments, then his voice filled me with calm.

"Dee, I'm so glad you called. How is your cousin?" He sounded out of breath. He must have run to the phone.

My hand gripped the receiver as if I was clinging to him. "Not good, I'm afraid. I'll need to stay with her for a while. Not long. The doctor said she doesn't have much time left."

"My God, Dee, I'm sorry." The genuineness in his voice eased my pain.

I wanted to tell him so many things, but would wait until when I returned to Rothmorton. "I'll keep you posted."

"It hasn't been the same without you here. I've missed you terribly."

"I miss everyone, too." My resistance to reveal my true feelings overcame my desperate need to be with him. Sometimes I didn't understand myself. "I'll call again next week. Okay?"

"Sure. What should I tell Ellen? She asks about you constantly."

"Tell her to keep up her lessons. I'll be quizzing her when I return." I laughed, yet the desire to cry almost overwhelmed me. "Tell her I miss her." My voice cracked.

"I will. Take care. If you need anything or to talk, I'm here for you."

I mumbled something stupid, hung up, and burst into tears. I missed him and yet I was glad for the distance.

"Someone special?" Daisy must have overheard my phone conversation. She stood in the kitchen doorway, holding a dish towel.

"No, my employer, H—Mr. Roth."

Daisy threw the towel over her shoulders and sat down. A sigh escaped her lips. "What's it like, your new job?"

"It's . . . different."

"In what way?"

"In every way." I heaved a sigh. "A whole other way of life. Exactly what I was looking for..."

"I hear a but in there somewhere." She narrowed her eyes at me. "You miss all these new people, don't ya'? I hear it in your voice. Not just the little girl, either."

"Oh Daisy, you were always so discerning. I'm confused."

"You like this Mr. Roth?"

"I do, but it's complicated, very complicated."

"How so?"

"Can't tell you right now. Secrets have recently come to light. It makes me feel . . . I don't know, mixed up."

"Sounds like it. Are they serious secrets?"

"To me, the secrets came as a shock. Coming here is a blessing in disguise. I have a lot to sort out. Can things be resolved? It remains to be seen. Strange things have been happening, disturbing things."

"Dangerous?" She sat up straight and shot me a worried look.

"Not directed at me, no, but possibly at Mr. Roth. We don't know who it is. Police are involved."

"What matters is that you are safe." Her kind eyes warmed my heart.

"I feel safe there. Don't you worry." I managed a small smile. Fatigued was overcoming me.

"You look tired, Dee. Go on to bed. I'll finish up in the kitchen."

"Good idea. Thanks for all your help."

**

It was a Sunday morning when Orpha passed away. I sat in the rocker in the corner of her room. Dozed off for a moment, it seemed. Two hours had passed when something jarred me awake. Not a sound, but a sense of relief and calm, and sadness filled the room. My sadness, as I looked at my cousin laying there. I knew her soul was gone.

Not a religious person, though I believed in a soul. All souls went to Heaven in my book. No one told me. Religion tells you there are only two places you can go, Heaven or Hell, and why I'm not religious. Orpha hadn't been very kind to me. She's all I had. It meant something, at least. Just me now. And there was work to be done.

Thankfully, before Orpha died, she opened up about her affairs and told me what she wanted. A simple burial, no funeral. Her will left everything to me and it stunned me. What a mysterious woman she was.

Not wanting to stay longer than necessary, I turned all the estate business over to a local attorney to sell everything. The attorney assured me he could accomplish everything by mail and phone and I shouldn't need to return.

**

The day before the burial, I went through the stuff in my room. Everything was still as I left it when I went to Rothmorton. A twin bed in the corner with a crocheted afghan I made in high school. I sat at the student desk by the window, going through the drawers. I found the usual writing tools, lined paper, pens, and a few photos, which I pulled out.

The one photo of my parents holding me when I was a baby, draped in a long white dress and knitted bonnet. They looked so happy. I barely remembered them. Dad worked long hours at the dairy farm down the road. Our farm had failed, and he sold most of the land. Mom kept the house together, cooking, cleaning, and doing odd sewing and mending jobs. It was post-depression and, like everyone else, they learned to scrimp and save.

One moonless night on a country road, a car without headlights swerved head-on into my parents' car. I survived somehow. I was in the hospital, the same room as my mother. One day, I woke up and her bed was empty. Dad had died in the crash, they said instantly. How do they know such things? They didn't give children time to grieve then. When I was well enough, they sent me away. Alone and surrounded by strangers. No one comforted me, no one tried to understand what I was experiencing. I cried myself to sleep every night for the first several weeks when I realized it wasn't temporary and no one would come for me.

I put their photo in an empty envelope and marked the outside simply: photos.

There was a photo of Orpha when she was younger, taken with her mother. Back when they still spoke to each other. I slipped it into the envelope.

The next photo I had cut out of the high school yearbook my sophomore year. Johnny Bash, captain of the football team, heartthrob of the senior class. I had a crush on him. The same as the other girls. He didn't know who I was. Being one of the shy kids, I kept to myself. Another photo paper-clipped to a newspaper article about him making a touchdown for an important game, and the headline read, "Most Likely to Succeed." I had heard nothing about him after he graduated. If he had become successful, it wasn't in McDonough County. I tossed the photo and article in the trash basket.

In the bottom drawer, under some notebooks, was my diary. I flipped through the pages in my childish scrawl and read some entries. There were a few where I truly put my feelings to paper. I barely managed those.

Burying my sadness and disappointments in life was easier than exposing them, even to myself. Writing poetry was the closest thing to divulging my feelings.

When I went to college, I was a butterfly bursting from the cocoon. I sat in the front row in the lectures and talked to people about serious subjects, literature, philosophy, current events, and even had a few dates with somewhat interesting boys. But I didn't fall in love with any of them.

I held the only things that had any meaning for me. Just two photos of the family now gone. I tossed the diary and the rest of the trash into an aluminum pail and lit them on fire. I didn't want them found. Not that they mattered. It was mostly a ritual of putting my past behind me.

There was nothing I wanted of Orpha's. She was a plain woman who lived a simple life with only the bare necessities. The rest inside the house was donated to charity or dumped. The value of the farm exceeded my imagination, even with the debts paid. Land still had value.

***

Only a few people attended the burial: Daisy, her husband and their two daughters, the attorney, a couple of neighbors from down the road, and Orpha's farm hand. Not even a minister there. What she wanted. Daisy and I said a few words. And it was over. Everyone dispersed, heading to wherever.

"You going back to Massachusetts?" Daisy asked.

"I have a life there now. There is nothing here," I said.

"I understand. Would you keep in touch? I've known you for years. It would seem strange to just have you disappear forever." Tears welled up in her eyes.

"Of course, Daisy. I'll write, send a Christmas card. You do the same. You were always kind to me and I'll never forget it. Thank you for being Orpha's friend. You were her only one."

We embraced one last time, and I left, though not without reservations. True, there was nothing left for me in Illinois. I questioned whether my future belonged at Rothmorton and possibly with Hugh. My feelings for him were undeniable and growing stronger whenever I came into proximity to him. Ellen's birthday party showed me how very different Hugh and I were through the eyes of those horrid snobby Chabots. They tried very hard to humiliate me in front of Hugh. They did not reflect on him, but they reflected the world he lived in. Our one date was magical and fairytale-like, not reality, and I knew it.

Orpha's words came back to haunt me and to hurt me. "You think you can change who you are by a fancy education and living in a mansion? You can't, Dee Dee, you are country folk, simple, just like me, just like your parents."

On one level, I knew she was wrong because of her narrow view of the world. On another level, I wondered if she was right. I shuddered, forcing myself to forget her words. She would not control my life from beyond the grave.

A part of my life was gone. If I wanted to move forward and be with Hugh, he had serious issues to resolve. I was not sure if I could overlook them. And there was Jane. She haunted me. Unlike Mr. Rochester, Hugh did not attempt marriage while his wife still lived. Although I believed briefly, he was married. He was not.

The question remains, would he have told me the truth about his wife, if Sylvi hadn't burst in and I heard her story? How far would he have taken it? What if I had slept with him before the truth came out? The fire burned in me whenever I was near him. I'd have to forgive Hugh to let that happen.

And then there were the attempts on Ellen and Hugh's lives. And the threatening notes. It scared me. It was all too much to handle. A decision needed to be made. I would make it at Rothmorton.

CHAPTER TWELVE

Three weeks had passed since I had left Rothmorton. Long enough to miss the people I had come to know and love. Ben waited for me at the train station and he was a welcomed sight. Again, I sat in the front seat. He grinned while putting my suitcase in the trunk.

"You look terrific Miss Danes. Time away has been good for you."

"Not really. It was very sad. My cousin passed away."

"Sorry for your loss, but I sure am glad you're back."

"Thanks. Tell me what you know?" Hoping for tidbits of news about Sylvi and Mr. Roth, wondering if anyone had overhead the horrid scene in the library and spreading rumors.

"Oh, the usual. Mr. Roth has been driving into Boston more. Nurse Clayton and Ellen are the same, though whenever I see Ellen, she asks when I'm going to get you. Nothing really new."

Surprised to hear Sylvi was still at Rothmorton, though Hugh had told me she was staying. I figured she would be uncomfortable after everything.

"Nothing terrible has happened again? No vandalism or attempts on Mr. Roth's life."

"Yeah, kinda quiet. More security, though, which is new. I bet you've really missed Mr. Roth?"

I tensed. What does Ben think he knows? I glanced at him. "I've missed everyone."

"Oh, come on, Miss Danes, I don't know about anyone else, but it's been pretty obvious to me you have a thing for him, and I think he's kinda sweet on you."

I didn't know what to say. Could I trust Ben? He seems to think he knows what I feel.

"Mr. Roth is a fine man."

"He sure is, but not what I mean."

"I enjoy his company."

"Oh, okay, if it's the way you wanna play it. I get it. Gotta keep things quiet, right? Worried about how things might look to others." He gripped the steering wheel tighter as the car curved around a bend. "Despite the evening in Boston."

I bit my lip to keep from acknowledging his comments. "It was a nice evening, except for the tire issue. So, you can believe whatever you want, Ben, but there's really nothing going on between Mr. Roth and me." I didn't lie. Nothing much had happened, except for the one passionate kiss.

He rolled his eyes at me. "Just so you know, I'm all for it. You and Mr. Roth are perfect for each other."

"You think so, huh?" It was a nice thing to hear. If Ben could see it, then maybe I was letting Orpha's negativity get the best of me. I had to remind myself there was more going on than the attraction between Hugh and me. A lot more.

Ben grinned at me again, and I laughed. The rest of the drive was relaxing and Ben chattered gossip about people I didn't know. We were almost to Rothmorton, and my excitement grew.

The moment the car pulled through the iron gates, a sense of home and happiness washed over me. There was much to face and accept. Tiny bits of doubt clouded my thoughts despite my happy state of mind.

It was a relief to learn Hugh wasn't home. He'd been working in Boston during the week. I wasn't ready to face him right away.

Once settled in, I sought Ellen in her room. It was empty and so was Sylvi's. I found Mrs. Chambers on the first floor in the morning room. She directed the maids in cleaning. The windows faced the east with only morning sun. With fall around the corner, it wouldn't be warm.

"Miss Danes, you've returned!" Mrs. Chambers threw her arms open. Her sincere smile welcomed me, and I couldn't resist giving her a hug. "What are you doing in here?"

"Mr. Roth wanted some rooms opened up. He didn't tell me why. I just do as I'm told."

"Where's Ellen? I missed her."

"She and Nurse Clayton went out into the garden." She turned to the window. "On the other side. I see them coming from the cliff walk. They finally finished working on the railing."

I thanked her and went out the door leading to the garden. They waved me over to where they took seats on the bench near the fishpond.

Ellen shouted my name, running toward me and threw her arms about my waist. "I'm so glad you're home. I've missed you so much. Nurse Clayton has been teaching me, but you're my real tutor."

"I've missed you too." I knew for sure I had fallen in love with her. She was so lovable.

"It's nice to see you," Sylvi said and mouthed an 'I'm sorry.' "Let's get together later to chat."

"Sure, after Ellen goes to bed, like we used to." My consternation about Sylvi made me tense. To continue working together, we needed to find a resolve. I wasn't looking forward to our chat.

***

It was Friday, and Hugh returned to the mansion for dinner. A quiet meal, except for Ellen telling her uncle all about her week. I spoke only when questioned. He and I would glance at each other casually. I was eager to talk to him alone. Dinner was over. We retired to the library for an hour of television. No change there. His eyes were on me more than the TV. I fidgeted with anticipation.

As soon as Ellen bid goodnight and she left with Sylvi, I exhaled a long sigh of relief. Hugh laughed and poured himself a brandy and me a glass of port.

"What's so funny?" I took the glass and sipped.

"I did the same thing. A sigh of relief. I couldn't wait to be alone with you." He moved over to the sofa to sit next to me, leaving about a foot between us.

I longed for his heat and energy, wanting to sit closer. "It's so good to see you, Hugh." And it was so good to call him by his first name.

His hand rested over mine.

"You look beautiful. Thanks for coming back. I wasn't sure you would."

"It gave me time to consider whether I would."

His smile vanished, replaced with a questioning look. "But you are here. Does this mean . . .?"

"This is my home now. There's nothing for me in Illinois."

"I'm sorry you had to go through it alone. Are you okay?"

"It was difficult, but also a release. Orpha was a hard woman, and she knew it and didn't care. All in the past now. I'm ready to move on. There are questions still on my mind."

"For me? About what?" His brandy was almost gone.

He must have been as nervous as I.

"About Nora. I know you suffered. Are you still grieving the loss of her?"

He blew out a long exhale, stretching his arms out as if he were releasing something. "Ah, the grief, and the guilt, too."

"Guilt?"

"The guilt over letting my father take control of Nora's situation. My not standing up to him. If I hadn't left her there, or took her somewhere else . . ."

"Since you don't know exactly what happened, I don't see you are to blame and shouldn't feel guilty."

"Maybe. And the grief. Oh yes, the loss was great."

"You loved her a lot, I'm sure."

"Deeply. She was my first love."

I wanted to ask if there had been anyone since. But kept it to myself. "Are you over it? I'm mean . . . do you still miss her?"

"Am I still in love with her? No. It passed years ago. All this business being dredged up again. Of course, old feelings have resurfaced. But I assure you, what I feel for you is real." His brows knitted together with worry.

"Just curious." Not sure whether I was telling the exact truth. He convinced me his old feelings for Nora wouldn't affect us.

"Good. I'd hate for you to think my past would get in the way of . . . this." His hand caressed my arm.

The tingling from his touch triggered my mouth into an involuntary smile. The question most on my mind hovered on my lips. "Right, and why I must ask you my next question." I shifted in my seat, my voice wavered, unsure if it was the right time.

"Anything. I promise to be completely honest."

"I've been wondering . . . if Sylvi hadn't burst in on us accusing you, forcing out the truth, would you have told me yourself?"

He avoided my eyes, glancing at the ceiling, then the window, then anywhere but directly at me. He pulled his hand away and stood, and paced, then turned to face me.

"It's a question I've been asking myself ever since you left. I've been living the lies for years. Being honest is the most important thing, especially now . . ."

His response was not what I expected. It really threw me. My whole body tensed, turning my stomach upside down.

"I'd like to believe I would have told you, eventually." He saw the look on my face. It must have been one of horror. He sat down next to me, close.

I recoiled. "I see. I certainly hope you would have. It's important to me you can be honest with me now and going forward."

"Oh Dee, I've told you everything. There are no more secrets. You must know I'm relieved everything came out. Even with the way it happened. The truth will come out publicly. I will take responsibility for the perpetuation of my father's lies. I just hope all this doesn't scare you off." His hand moved to touch mine, then stopped.

"The truth does need to be told. However, when is not my decision, whatever my feelings are. I dread when it happens. Because it will hurt people, Ellen, for one." My arms ached to hold him, yet I did nothing. Still, I resisted giving in completely.

"I'm glad you understand."

"This place is more like home than anywhere."

"I feel a 'but' coming."

The look on his face tore me up inside. I had to be honest, though it could ruin everything. "Thinking you might not have told me the truth—makes me question who you are." My words dropped like lead in the air. The pain in his eyes cut me to my core. My heart tightened.

"You know who I am, Dee."

"I thought I did."

"What can I do to convince you?" His eyes grew wide.

"Not sure. I thought about you a great deal and missed you so much. I wanted more with you."

"And now?"

"I just need more time. Can you understand?"

A deathly awkward silence sat between us for several moments. I held my breath.

"Regretfully, yes, I understand." His shoulders slumped.

I breathed again. "Do you really?" A sincere smile spread across my face, wanting to ease the pain I was causing him.

He nodded and perked up. "I need to set things right, with you, with Ellen, and those who believed the lies for so many years." He crinkled his brow and those brilliant blue eyes clouded over.

"How?"

"Not sure yet. I have a meeting with my lawyers to find out if I've broken any laws."

"I hadn't thought of that. I hope not."

"Yeah, me too. Having you here beside me gives me strength."

"Even though I can't give you more right now?"

"I'm glad you're here, and you will bear with me while I figure it out."

"I'm not going anywhere . . . for now."

He flinched at my words. How long I would wait remained to be seen.

His hand covered mine, and I didn't move. Looking down, I realized we had gradually drawn closer to each other to avoid anyone overhearing our conversation. Our faces were just inches away. My heart beat quickly, thinking he was going to kiss me, but he moved away. I longed to feel his lips on mine, yet relieved he didn't. I was in turmoil, and kissing him would only confuse me more.

He stood and clasped his hands behind him, acting more like my employer and less like the hopeful suitor, his voice superficial. It was my turn to flinch.

"As I told you on the phone, the fingerprint report from the police cleared all the staff from the investigation. With the heightened security, there have been no recent incidences. I wished I knew what it was about."

The mood had turned awkward again. I cleared my throat, swallowing hard. "I feel safer, and I'm sure everyone else does."

"Good. I want you to feel safe."

The library door opened, and it was Sylvi. "Excuse me, Hugh. Is this a good time, Dee?"

It was strange hearing Sylvi call him Hugh. They certainly had worked through their issues. Why can't I do the same?

"I'll call it a night," he said. "Have a good evening." Nodding to each of us, he left.

Our conversation so abruptly ended, there was barely time to pull myself together for my visit with Sylvi. She didn't act as if anything were out of the ordinary, for which I was grateful.

Sylvi's hands shook with apparent nervousness when she took the club chair next to the sofa. Unsure what to say, I waited for her to begin.

"Let me first apologize for my outburst with Hugh in front of you that day. It was terrible timing and I hope you'll forgive me." Her dark eyes glistened with remorse.

"Why, with me in the room? It was a conversation meant between you two."

"You're right. It should have been private. I believed Nora was alive and still married to Hugh, despite the rumors about their marriage being annulled. It was partly for your benefit, so you wouldn't get sucked into more of his lies."

"It backfired on you because you had it wrong and I became collateral damage."

"Can you forgive me? Even though it's a lot to ask."

"I thought we were friends. You encouraged me to get involved with him. Why?"

"Oh that. I believed in the lie that the marriage was annulled. I was trying to find out where she went. It never occurred to me he did anything wrong."

"But you did."

"Yes, that day I had just learned Nora and Hugh's marriage wasn't annulled. I was angry and wanted to protect you."

"A strange way to protect me."

"I shouldn't have been so harsh. After you ran out of here, I got some very hard blows of truth. I truly believed he was hiding her somewhere, certainly not dead." Her eyes glistened with unshed tears.

Seeing her in pain and suffering a loss softened my heart.

"Well . . . I probably should thank you for bursting in the way you did. I believed Hugh had annulled his marriage, like everyone else. Though, when I first arrived, I thought he was unmarried. Until I heard rumors in town."

"Didn't Mrs. Chambers give you the warning about his wife?"

"No. I discovered it quite by accident."

"How odd. You ran out of here so upset and in shock, I didn't expect you to return. Believe me, I feel awful about it."

"Hugh found me and explained everything, I mean every—thing. I'm glad you stayed. Ellen would have missed you terribly. It was a terrible way for you to find out about your sister's death. The whole situation is tragic."

"Yes, tragic is the right word. I wish we knew what really happened to her. I should have been here for her. Her depression and attempted suicide? Something horrible happened to her as a POW. And the military does nothing for nurses who suffer."

"What do you mean? They provide help for the soldiers."

"Sure for the men. They think nurses can handle it as part of our work. For God's sake, we're human too. The tragedies of war are despicable, and being a prisoner would be insurmountable. I'm surprised more nurses didn't wig out."

"What about you? Didn't you have similar experiences? Not as a prisoner. Triaging the wounded must have been extremely stressful."

Sylvi paused for a moment to collect herself, taking a deep breath and pulling a hanky from her pocket, wiping her tears. "I worked in a large hospital in France, after the Germans had left. They were postwar rehabilitation wards. I wasn't in a combat zone and I didn't leave until '48. It was bad enough, seeing the injuries soldiers sustained were horrible."

"You and your sister did important work for our country. I thank you for your service and sorry for what the two of you suffered."

Sylvi managed a smile of thanks.

"However, yours and Hugh's deceptions have been hard for me."

"I know. Lying isn't easy for me. Yet, you've forgiven Hugh?"

I hesitated answering, for I forgave him with reservations. Sylvi hadn't earned the right for that detail. "Mostly, I have."

"And for me?"

"I'm working on it. Rothmorton is my home and I want to be happy here."

"Glad to hear it."

"Ellen still doesn't know, I assume." My feelings toward Sylvi had an enormous question mark. I had thought we'd become friends, but she, too, was a master at deception.

"Dear no, she doesn't. I agree with Hugh. We should wait a few years before she knows everything. We'll tell her I'm her aunt, soon."

"Good." Even in a few years, it will be difficult for Ellen to understand.

"You need time to adjust to all the revelations from me and Hugh. I hope someday you can find it in your heart to forgive both of us." Sylvi clutched her hands together as though she were praying.

"I want us to be friends again." I meant it, but didn't know how long it would take.

"Me too. You were gone for a while. Did you go home?"

"My cousin was ill. She died. I came back." It's all I could muster. Everything was so fresh, tears welled and I turned away.

"My condolences. I wasn't aware."

"Hugh didn't tell you?" My tears were not about Orpha. It was all the emotion returning to Rothmorton. I brushed away my tears and faced her.

"He didn't tell anyone anything, only you would return when you could."

"Yes, he's good at keeping secrets."

"Dee, I sort of understand his side. I can't imagine what kind of man Hugh's father was to have taken such drastic measures. I'm positive our Hugh is not like his father, despite his perpetuating the lies for so long."

"I hope not." My terseness was unintended, but I was not ready to talk about the whole sordid tale. At least, not with Sylvi, not yet.

"I've agreed to keep everything to myself, until he can figure out how to set things straight," Sylvi said.

"With a long history of the lie, it won't be easy for him to come clean."

"I'm sure."

"What was Nora was like? There aren't photos of her around the house."

"I noticed. I have a little one I carry with me always." She pulled a chain around her neck up from under her uniform, a locket. "I'm touched by your interest. Here."

I took the locket from her and opened it. A tiny black-and-white image of a pretty young girl with light hair and a brilliant smile. "She was lovely." I gave it back to her.

"She was just eighteen. I was fourteen then. I idolized her flamboyant, independent ways, wanting adventure and excitement. When the war came, she enlisted as soon as she could." She took a tissue from her pocket.

"I'm so sorry, Sylvi. Didn't mean for you to cry."

"Oh, crying is something I do whenever I think of Nora. Now even more when I think of what happened to her." She sniffled and squared her shoulders, sitting up straight. "Anyway, there's something else I wanted to share with you. My husband is moving to Plymouth."

"Hugh told me. I know now who you were talking to that day."

"What day?"

"I accidentally overhead you talking on the phone the day we went on the yacht. I wondered who was pressuring you about getting information."

"You heard, did you? And that's why you thought I was the one vandalizing, killing cats, and trying to hurt Ellen and Hugh."

We both chuckled in embarrassment.

"Glad it wasn't you. When is he moving here?"

"As soon as he can tie up some business in Manhattan. Hopefully, before Thanksgiving. I don't want to leave Ellen, and he is a very understanding man."

"You're lucky."

"I am. We met in the service, too." She paused a moment. "I'm glad we had this talk."

I smiled.

"I should check on Ellen."

"I'll stay a few moments more. Good night."

We clasped hands together briefly, and she left the library.

If it wasn't Sylvi doing all those terrible things, who was?

***

The days passed without event. Hugh had increased security by hiring additional guards to canvass the property. Though I felt safer, the police continued to search for a suspect on the brake issue and the vandalism.

A tall, muscular guard assigned to the perimeter of the house during the day strolled through the garden while I sat in my favorite spot, writing in my notebook. He tipped his hat, and I smiled politely. We never spoke, but his presence comforted me.

Charlie came along to work on some shrubs nearby. He greeted me and began trimming a bush.

"How are you today, Charlie?"

Charlie raised up from his task. "Mighty fine to see you, Miss Danes. I be doing well."

"I've been meaning to thank you for the flowers I found in my room my first day back from my trip."

"Welcome, ma'am. Probably the last of the season. Fall is coming."

"True. You've worked for the Roths a long time."

"Yes, ma'am."

"Did you know Mr. Roth's wife?" I figured it would be alright to ask.

"Been on this land since Mr. Hugh's father was a boy. True enough. Didn't know Mrs. Roth, personal like, before she left. Heard tell how sweet and kind she was. Then she gone."

"Did you know why she left?"

"Learned long time ago not to ask questions."

"Mr. Roth's father was a stern taskmaster, I've been told."

"As a man, he was so. As a boy, me and him played together. My mama worked in the kitchen."

"Really? I wondered, because you don't seem old enough to have been an adult then. Have you ever wanted to live elsewhere?"

He resumed trimming the bush while talking. "My late wife wanted to leave."

"You were married?" Another surprise. Even Mrs. Chambers didn't tell me.

He nodded. "My son served in the war with Mr. Hugh."

"Your son? Does he work here?" I put my notebook in my bag. Talking to Charlie was much more interesting than my writing.

"Oh, no, ma'am. My boy went to college, thanks to Mr. Hugh."

"You mean Mr. Roth paid for his tuition? What about the G.I. Bill? Isn't it intended to help veterans go to college?"

Charlie shifted from one foot to the other and wiped his brow. "Well . . . he applied, like a lotta others, just like us. Didn't get the grant."

"What do you mean, just like us?"

"Negroes, ma'am. The G.I. Bill goes first to the Whites. The way things is. But Mr. Hugh, he comes through. Pays for my boy's schoolin'. An accountant in Boston now." He beamed with pride.

"How wonderful. I didn't know the government played favorites with service benefits. Seems unfair to me."

"You are a rare person, Miss Danes, just like Mr. Hugh. I best be gettin' back to my work, ma'am."

"Thank you for your story, Charlie. It's nice to hear good things about Mr. Roth."

I packed up my things and strolled out along the cliff walk. It was the first time since Hugh and I almost went over the cliff. The railing was all new and included mesh barriers from the rail to the ground, making it safer. Cold wind blew off the ocean. I buttoned my sweater up to my neck and sat on the nearest bench.

Charlie's story encouraged me. Hugh helped Charlie's son to set an unjust matter straight. It reminded me of his kindness toward Ben in giving him a job. Hugh was an enigma. It was important to trust him to follow through on his promises. We both needed time.

CHAPTER THIRTEEN

It was Saturday. Not hungry, I arrived downstairs after breakfast, hoping for a quiet cup of coffee in the morning room to write. Camped in the foyer, Mr. Greene worked on Hugh's portrait. He said the room had better light, what with the skylight in the ceiling on the third floor. A feature I had not noticed before. I peeked in on the process a few times, but today, my alone time beckoned.

They had transformed the morning room since the cleaning. New potted plants flanked the large window. Species I had not seen before, like the tall thick leafed rubber plant, voluminous ferns, and palms. It seemed a waste, since the fall was upon us with cooler weather. Once winter hit, the plants might die, unless they bring in heaters.

The entire effect was exotic, giving a delicious sereneness to the room. I particularly enjoyed the Italian rattan peacock chair. It made me feel like a queen with its large, round backrest. My request for a radio was granted. One sat on the table next to my chair by the window. The morning sun filtered in, while I tuned the radio to the soothing sounds of Chopin's Nocturne in E flat.

After a sip of coffee, I opened my notebook. My poems no longer dwelled on unrequited love. Not since my awakened emotions over Hugh. The words spilled across the page without effort and the time fled by.

Sylvi and Ellen entered from the back stairs. Ellen was wearing her birthday party dress. She twisted side to side to make a swishing sound.

"Miss Danes, guess what?" She bounced into the rattan chair next to me.

"Good morning. You're very excited about something. I can't guess. Tell me." I glanced at Sylvi, hoping for a hint, and she put her finger to her lips, not wanting to interrupt Ellen.

"I'm going to be painted."

"A portrait?"

"Just like Uncle Hugh." She smiled with her usual gleeful disposition, lifting my spirits as she does each day in our lessons.

"How fun. When?"

"Today. Will you come and watch?"

"You bet I will. Oh, that's why you're wearing your party dress?"

"Uh-huh. Come now. Please?" She fluttered her eyelashes, framing her brilliant blue eyes. Oh boy, she would be a heart-breaker one day.

"Okay." I put my pen in my jacket pocket and picked up the notebook.

Together, we marched down the hall toward the foyer. Hugh was wearing a dark blue business suit and sitting in an antique wooden throne chair with his knees crossed. He wore a solemn expression which broke as soon as he saw Ellen running toward him.

She jumped into his lap.

"I'm ready for my painting."

Mr. Green stopped painting and frowned. "Ellen, what did your uncle tell you about disturbing his pose? I'm not ready for you yet."

"I'm sorry." She thrust her lower lip out into a pout.

"Now, now, Ellen, no pouting. Go sit in the chair over there. Miss Danes, Nurse Clayton, you too. Just be quiet until Mr. Greene is done with me."

Sylvi had already dragged in side chairs from the parlor and we sat quiet as mice, except Ellen, who squirmed impatiently. I tried to hide my amusement, not wanting to encourage her.

Hugh was doing the same.

"Mr. Roth, please don't change your expression. I'm working on your mouth right now."

Hugh pulled a straight face, and we all sat still. It was very interesting to watch, however. I had always wanted to learn to paint, but writing was more my speed. The painting was so lifelike. It was difficult to tell the painting from the real person. After an hour, Mr. Greene stepped back and put down his palette and brush.

"It's not done, but this stage needs to be completely dry before I do the finishing touches. In the meantime, we can decide where Miss Ellen will be setup. Any suggestions, Mr. Roth."

Hugh tilted his head to think. I raised my hand to catch his attention.

"Miss Danes? You have a suggestion?"

"How about the morning room? She could sit in the big rattan chair surrounded by the plants."

Mr. Greene nodded. "Sounds interesting. Let's go have a look. I would like a brighter room for her, especially in the lovely white dress she's wearing."

Ellen jumped up and started to run.

"No running. What have I told you?" Hugh said.

"Walk like a lady, like I showed you," Sylvi said.

Ellen stopped and then restarted walking very prim and proper with her arms out and her chin up. She made me want to laugh, but I held it in.

We all trailed through the house. Mr. Green surveyed the space, moving chairs around and checking the light.

"I don't remember the light this bright the first time I looked at it. Surprising, since it's later in the year."

"I think they washed the windows," Hugh said.

"Of course. That would change the light," Mr. Greene said. "The plants are perfect. Ellen, sit in this chair, please." He pointed to the peacock chair. "We'll need another pillow for her, but I think this works. Thank you, Miss Danes, for the suggestion."

"Oh, Ellen, you look divine. I can hardly wait to see the portrait when it's completed," I said.

"I agree," said Hugh.

Having to sacrifice my favorite spot for Ellen's portrait was a small price to pay to see her so excited.

Mr. Greene came twice a week, working on both portraits. I found it fascinating to watch him work, mixing the colors and measuring. He said it was very important to ensure an exact likeness. The painting looked just like Hugh.

The first time Ellen sat for him, her excitement almost ruined the sitting.

"Ellen, please sit still," Hugh said.

"It's all right," Mr. Green said. "Children are a challenge to paint, but she'll settle down . . . eventually."

I sent a stern look at Ellen, and she stopped fidgeting. Hugh noticed and whispered, "Amazing. Magic?"

"Practice," I said. "How do you think I get her to focus on her lessons?"

He nodded his approval and slipped out of the room. I assumed he went to the library. But I saw him through the window speaking to the security guard. It was difficult to act as though everything was normal when it was not. As long as Ellen didn't notice, was all that mattered.

Hugh had mentioned nothing to me recently about the ongoing police investigation, though it was constantly on my mind.

Was it a lull before the storm?

***

The days got shorter. The leaves were falling, and the evenings were colder.

One of the most prestigious families in the Plymouth area invited Ellen to a children's Halloween party. It was all she talked about and a challenge keeping her focused on her lessons.

"If you pay attention today, I'll make you a costume. Who shall you be for the party?"

"Oh, goody." She clapped her hands together and pounded her feet on the floor.

"Calm down, please."

"I want to be a fairy. Can you make me a fairy?"

Oh boy, it would be tricky and a stretch of my skills. "Well . . . I can try."

"Oh, please Miss Danes, pretty please. I'll help."

Her adorable face had lit up the room and my heart melted. I couldn't let her down. There was enough time before the party. Though I needed to look for patterns in town.

"All right, Ellen, back to your lessons."

"O—kay." Ellen moped and picked up her pencil, making marks at a snail's pace.

"I think you can copy the sentence a little faster, don't you think?" I rolled my eyes and smiled secretly.

***

Becky and I had promised to have lunch one day, so I called the café and we planned for my next day off. I rode a bicycle to town since the weather was still nice during the day. We met at the little deli on Main Street and took our sandwiches to Elder Brewster Gardens. She carried our food while I pushed my bike along. It was a bright sunny day, and we chit chatted about different things until she turned it personal.

"You mentioned you had gone home for a while. Did something happen?"

"My cousin was ill." I paused, unsure whether Becky was trustworthy. There wasn't anyone I wanted to confide in at Rothmorton.

"Is she okay now?"

"She died."

"I'm terribly sorry." Becky sounded sincere.

"I also needed time away . . . to think about things and my life. You know."

"Oh, don't I ever. Let's sit by the pond." Becky spread a picnic blanket on the ground while I found a place to park the bike. We sat on the blanket to eat our lunch. Becky wore sunglasses, and she had touched up the dark roots, making her appear younger.

"Something happening with your job you're unsure about?" Becky said.

"Um, sort of, but it's being worked out now, I think."

"You like the little girl, don't you?"

"She's truly delightful. I'm going to make her a Halloween costume, a fairy."

"How sweet of you. I never learned to sew."

"Do you have hobbies?"

"Nah."

"What about seeing the world?" It seemed like she didn't really want to share about herself.

"Oh sure, takes money, though. Won't happen on my wages." She tossed her blond curls and laughed. "Unless I meet a rich man."

What irony. I had met a rich man, and his money didn't solve the problems. Money made it possible for him to perpetuate them.

"You dating anyone in town?" I asked.

"Being a waitress, I meet everyone. All kinds. Some young. Some old. No one in particular. You?"

"I don't get out much to meet anyone. No time for dating either."

"Word is Mr. Roth might have found someone."

"People are talking?"

Becky laughed. "You know how people gossip. Don't know if it's true. You'd know better than me." She looked at me with narrowed eyes. "Do you know?"

"How would I know?" I turned to gaze at the swans in the pond, uncomfortable at the turn in the conversation. "It's pretty here."

"Yeah."

"This was a marvelous idea, Becky. We should do it again."

"Sure. Let's."

We basked in the sun until Becky left for an afternoon shift. I headed back to Rothmorton, taking my time. Wanting solitude, I turned left at the fork away from the house. The density of the woods broke into a clearing with a narrow path. It was level enough for the bike. I followed it until I reached an iron fence enclosure and a gate. I pushed the bike up to the gate to peer inside. There were little bouquets of flowers set in vases around a manicured lawn. A cemetery. Was it where Nora's buried? A chill passed through me. Leaning the bike against the fence I pushed open the unlocked gate, taking care where I stepped. I hated the thought of walking over someone's grave.

There were several headstones, flat on the ground, nothing fancy like tall pillars or monuments, like in some cemeteries. More like the one I had done for Orpha, but marble, or granite, and very thick, rising from the ground about five inches with elaborate engravings with flowers or angels. The first one I came upon was Hugh's grandfather with his wife next to him. Next to hers was a small one decorated with cherubs. It must have been a child. The years were only five apart from birth to death. Ellen was only a year older. If anything happened to her, I would be devastated.

In the corner was a lone marker. Nora's. A strangeness overcame me at finding her buried in the same place as the man who kept her death a secret. I grieved for her pain and for Hugh's. The whole situation weighed on me. As I turned and walked back to the entrance, Hugh's parents' graves were in front of me. I stopped cold.

I had not understood at first what Hugh experienced, his losing a wife, his father's oppressive behavior and the fear of scandal. Perhaps it wasn't so different from my life, one filled with oppression and subjugation by those who controlled my life. If I had been in his situation, would have I done differently? I would like to think I would. But to be honest with myself, I did not know.

I would not have liked Mr. Roth Sr. and wondered what it must have been like for Nora. Poor Nora, suffering from the horrors of war, she came to this house only to end up in an asylum. What happened to her there? Was it a patient or someone on staff? Was she raped? I shuddered at the thought. Whoever it was, it ended badly with her death. Ellen was the light coming from such a dark place.

I hurried out of there, riding as fast as I could to the mansion. Avoiding speaking to anyone as I passed through the lower level and up the backstairs to my room. I spent the rest of the afternoon alone writing poetry. Putting thoughts and emotions into poetry gave me peace.

CHAPTER FOURTEEN

It was late one night in the sewing room, and I had completed the fairy dress. There was still time to work on the wings, which were mostly handwork, not needing the machine. I put the dress in a special box and went down the backstairs. I heard someone running down the second-floor hall. Not again. When I reached the hallway, it was empty, except for the guard sitting outside of Ellen's door.

The guard's head was resting against the wall. I went down to ask him if he had seen anyone. When I reached him, his eyes were closed.

"Excuse me," I said in a whisper.

He didn't move, so I touched his arm and his eyes jerked open.

"Miss Danes?"

"Mr. Thomas, were you asleep?"

"I'm sorry, it won't happen again."

"I heard someone running down this hall as I came down the back stairs. But I didn't see anyone. I hoped you did."

"Uh, I didn't hear anyone."

"Not if you were asleep," I said. "I'll need to tell Mr. Roth."

He nodded and sat up straight, his eyes wide awake. A little late, though.

When I entered my room, the hint of cheap perfume hung in the air. It wasn't mine. The same shiver returned as I switched on the light and surveyed the room. Everything was in place, except the bag of supplies for the wings wasn't on the boudoir chair. I searched the wardrobe, bathroom, chiffonier, but it was gone. "What the heck?"

Heavy bags under my eyes greeted me in the mirror the next morning. I didn't care. I needed to talk to Hugh. It gave me the creeps someone had been in my room. Who would have taken Ellen's costume?

He was outside in the garden, smoking under the arbor. The leaves had already dropped from the roses winding around the trellis.

"Here you are." I hurried toward him.

He turned and flashed one of his fabulous smiles. "You look tired."

"I am. Worked late last night on Ellen's costume."

"You didn't have to do that. I would have bought a costume for her."

"She wanted to help design it. I enjoy sewing and making things."

"It's the creative side of you I adore." He dropped his cigarette and snuffed it out with his shoe. "Sorry about the smoke. Would love to kiss you right now."

I ignored his comment, my mind focused. "Something's happened again."

"Not possible. We have guards everywhere."

"I'm sure someone's been in my room and took the materials I'd left for Ellen's costume."

"Are you sure you didn't leave them somewhere else?"

"Positive. I smelled perfume in the room right after I heard someone running in the hall as I came down the backstairs. It's someone on the estate. Who else?"

"Was the guard outside Ellen's room?"

"He was there. Asleep. I woke him and, of course, he didn't hear anyone."

"Asleep? Damn. Which guard?"

"Mr. Thomas. This is very upsetting. What if this person got into Ellen's room while the guard was asleep?"

"I'll take care of the guard. The fingerprints didn't show a match on any of the staff." He ran his hand through his hair. "This has got to stop."

"Anyone on the property at that hour of the night would be on staff, right?"

"What time was it?"

"After midnight."

"I'll have the property watchman check who was here last night. Not everyone lives here, you know. But if it's a woman, leaves only a few to interrogate."

"Interrogate? Is that necessary?"

"We need to investigate this, Dee."

"But Ellen will find out. That's the last thing we need. Don't you agree?"

"Yes." He crossed his arms. His brow furrowed, thinking. "I'll speak to the inspector. Maybe they can investigate quietly."

"This makes me really uncomfortable. I can replace the materials. No harm done."

"Well . . . We could call it a prank and forget about it. I'll still have the records checked who was on the property last night."

"Okay. We'll find out who it is. I'm sure."

"In the meantime, keep your door locked."

"What about the laundry maid?"

"Let Mrs. Chambers deal with it." He reached for my hand and squeezed it, without looking around to make sure no one saw, and kissed me for a second.

I wanted more, but gently pushed him away. "Thanks. I needed that."

***

The party was on the twenty-fourth, the Saturday before Halloween. Despite the loss of materials for the fairy wings, I found suitable substitutions in the sewing room and completed Ellen's costume in time. I carried the dress and wings down to Ellen's room and knocked. Sylvi opened the door.

"Miss Danes, come on in. Ellen is beyond excited."

As soon as I stepped inside, Ellen rushed up to give me a big hug. "Oh, you're here. Let me see, let me see!"

"Now calm down Ellen, or you'll work yourself up and start coughing," Sylvi said.

"Exactly. Let's change you into the costume," I said.

Ellen jumped up and down, giggling and clapping her hands.

Once she settled down, Sylvi took Ellen's day clothes off, and I helped to get her camisole and panties on.

"First goes the petticoats. Not as many as your birthday dress, because the costume needs to flow and flutter like a fairy."

"How many?" Ellen said.

Three, and here is the last one. I held up the dress made of pink satin and tulle.

"I love it," Ellen said. Her eyes sparkled like diamonds.

"Arms up again." The dress slipped right over her head and fell over the petticoats perfectly. "Now the wings. I made them from wire coat hangers and tulle and made two loops attached in the middle. These are tricky. Goes on like a harness." Explaining more for Sylvi. Ellen just wanted to wear it. She didn't care how I made it.

"It's lovely, Dee, you are so handy. I could never make something like this," Sylvi said.

"Thanks, and the last piece." Out of my bag, I retrieved the wand with a star at the end.

"A fairy wand? Oh, Thank you, Miss Danes. I love it."

"I sure hope Mr. Roth has a camera downstairs to take pictures. She won't look like this by the time she gets home."

We both laughed as Ellen twirled around and around, touching toys in her room with the wand like it had magic.

"It's time to go downstairs."

It was a daytime party, so the guard wasn't in the house. Mr. Roth had arranged for a policewoman to attend with Sylvi as just another staff person. Ellen wasn't aware she was being guarded. She lived in a bubble of happiness and what we all wanted for her.

Hugh and Mrs. Chambers were waiting in the foyer as we descended the stairs, reminiscent of the birthday party without the throngs of people.

"My goodness, don't you look just like a fairy," Mrs. Chambers said.

"Ellen, sweetheart, you look beautiful. Now stay on the stairs. I've got the camera right here."

No one needed to tell Ellen to pose. She was already leaning on the banister, holding her wand out like a fairy. She turned so he could capture the wings in the photos.

Watching the two of them touched me deeply. My childhood did not have people who loved me, protected me, and made me feel safe. It filled my heart with happiness for Ellen, and I wanted it to last. I dreaded the day when she would learn the truth about her mother.

"Miss Danes," Hugh said, "You are a wonder. This costume is amazing."

I flashed him an appreciative smile.

Behind Mrs. Chambers was the plainclothes policewoman dressed in one of the maid's uniforms. They introduced her to Ellen, then left with Ben driving the Bentley.

We stood at the entrance waving to them as the car moved around the fountain and down the drive.

"I thought you were going to the party, too." I turned to Hugh.

"Uh, me and fifty screaming children? Nope, I'd rather spend it with you."

"What will we do, hang around here?"

"Nope. Go change into something comfortable and bring a jacket. I'm driving."

I must have given him a look.

"Ben checked out the brakes this morning. We're good to go."

"Good. I'll be right back." I hurried back up to my room and changed into a pair of slacks and a lightweight pullover sweater, my new deck shoes, and a jacket. The days were still comfortable to wear regular clothes, but I needed to finish those two wool skirts I was making for myself before November got going.

I wore a scarf like a head band letting my hair fall loose assuming we were going in his Mercedes-Benz Roadster. I hoped the top was up, but I had something to tie my hair back, just in case. When I returned to the foyer, Mrs. Chambers was waiting for me at the open door.

"I hope you two have a lovely day," she said.

"Do you know where we are going?"

"He's very secretive today."

It wasn't something I wanted to hear. More secrets were the last thing I needed. Our first time completely alone. No Ben, no mansion with people. I should have been nervous.

Hugh stood next to the roadster. The top was up, thankfully. I grinned as he helped me into the car and then settled into the driver's seat.

"Am I the first woman you've taken for a spin in this roadster?"

"Of course. Who else?"

"How about MaryLou? She seemed to think you had promised her."

"Now you're the one who sounds jealous." He laughed.

"Perhaps." I giggled. "So, where are you taking me without a chaperone, Mr. Roth?"

"What's this, Mr. Roth business?" He chuckled.

"Just teasing. Really, where are we going?"

"Martha's Vineyard. This is probably the last chance we have before winter hits. You'll love it."

"What is it?"

"An island off the coast of Cape Cod."

"Sounds divine."

The drive down the coast to Woods Hole on Cape Cod proved to be uneventful and delicious at the same time. Nothing was going to ruin our second date. The sun shone brightly, with a few puffs of clouds in a vivid blue sky. What could be more perfect? Hugh hummed along with Bing Crosby on the radio while I gazed out the window at the gold, orange, and red landscape.

"Are you happy?" He threw me a sidelong glance.

"Very happy. It's a glorious day."

"And it's just beginning."

Hugh turned the car onto a familiar road.

"This is the way to the hospital."

"We go through there to get to Woods Hole to take a ferry across the channel."

"How fun."

The Harbor came into view. Hugh drove through the entrance directly onto the Islander ferry, large enough to carry freight trucks. He explained it was the first drive-through boat built for service to Martha's Vineyard. We spent the forty-five-minute crossing exploring the boat and sitting on the top deck.

He draped his arm about my shoulders. "Are you cold?"

"A bit, but I like the brisk air." I snuggled into his shoulder as he tightened his grip.

"It's a shame we didn't come during the summer when it was warmer, but it would have been ten times more crowded."

"I'm loving this and glad not to battle any crowds. Being with you makes me happy."

"Me, too," he said, taking my hand. "I've been meaning to tell you. I had a guard do a discreet room check, searching for the missing fairy costume materials.

"You did? And . . ."

"Nothing. The materials have vanished. No evidence, no one to blame."

"How odd. Could they have tossed the materials out?"

"They checked all the trash. Nothing."

"Whoever did it knew how to clear their tracks."

"Enough about that. Let's focus on enjoying this glorious day." He waved a hand in the air.

"Agreed!"

Hugh had plenty to talk about. I enjoyed listening to him share the history of the island and where he would take me. When the boat docked, we hurried back to the car, driving off the ferry and into the little town.

"There's a great pub nearby. You up for fish and chips?"

"Definitely."

After a leisurely lunch, he drove around the nearby area, pointing out the local landmarks and the lagoon to Oak Bluffs.

"Wait till you see the Gingerbread Houses."

"What are those?" I had no sooner said the words, I saw them, dozens of brightly painted cottages in rows close together, each structure a different color. "Oh my, how adorable they are."

"Let's take a walk." He parked and jumped out of the roadster and around to open my door for me. Taking my hand, we strolled through the park. "In the 1800s, a Methodist congregation came to the Vineyard for summer religious camps. They started out as tents, but over the years they built these cottages in what's called Carpenter's Gothic."

"They are amazing, so intricate are the carved pillars and ornamental railings and decorations. Almost like candy."

"Hence, the Gingerbread Houses."

"Oh, I get it now. Cute."

We continued walking away from the cottages to a shady spot under a tree.

"I love this." I stared out across the campground. There weren't many people around.

"I love . . ." Hugh stopped and turned me around to face him. "You."

"You . . ." I thought maybe I misheard him.

"Don't look so flustered. It can't possibly be a surprise to you." His hand brushed against my cheek.

"Yes, uh, I mean, wonderful." I held my breath, not knowing what else to say. Caught up in all the wonder of the day, so fairytale magical. It all felt unreal.

His face lit up, looking relieved. "Good and you?" There was an expectant tone in his words.

"My feelings run deep for you . . ." Why couldn't I say the words?

"There's a but coming, right?"

"Oh gosh. You are so romantic, and handsome, and . . ." I laughed again.

"Rich?" He laughed.

"Yes, but don't think . . . well, perhaps it does. I don't know if I belong in your world, not to mention what's happened lately. And there are those threats hanging over our heads."

"Sure, I understand." His face drooped as he took my hands in his. "I'm going to make things right in time. You belong in my world, trust me. I know, I know, it's probably a tall order, what with the deception. You've awakened feelings in me I thought were lost. Do you believe me?"

"I do. You are offering me your love. Something no one's done before. It's a mystery to me." My hesitation baffled me.

His body pressed against me until the hardness of the tree stopped me. His hands moved up my arms softly caressing them. A fire deep within me surged. He cupped my face, his eyes piercing mine, and I melted into his powerful chest.

"Kiss me." The words escaped my mouth with an urgent sigh.

There was no one around to watch or judge or threaten. It was just us, alone under a tree, when his lips captured mine and the world no longer existed. I was in the moment and enthralled. Oh, how I wanted to be in love. It was a long, penetrating kiss consuming me. Then he kissed my cheeks, my eyes, my forehead, and my lips again.

"God, you taste good."

I moaned. "Hm, you are a wonder."

"So are you."

"I don't want to leave this perfect place."

He pulled me away from the tree and enveloped me in his arms. I thought my knees would buckle.

We spent the rest of the afternoon holding hands, snuggling, and making out in his roadster. When Hugh realized the time, we rushed to catch the last ferry to Woods Hole. We almost didn't make it.

We returned to Rothmorton minutes before Ellen, Sylvi, and the policewoman.

Ellen wanted to tell us all about it in one breath. I worried she would get herself worked up and have another episode, but she was fine. The rest of the evening, Hugh and I would glance at each other with the slightest smiles, and each time, my heart would beat a little faster. I'd almost forgotten someone had been in my room stealing Ellen's costume. Someone who wished harm to Hugh and Ellen. But I did remember, and my skin prickled.

CHAPTER FIFTEEN

After Hugh had expressed his love for me, it was difficult to act as though nothing had happened. In fact, it was impossible. How could I pretend? I was no actress. Deception did not come easily to me. Every time we were in a room with other people, he stared at me and it was all I could do to ignore him, though it was possible I was staring back.

Sylvi may have caught on. Though she acted as though nothing had changed. I wanted to confide in her, but I needed more time to trust her again.

Ben drove me into town on my next day off. I rode in the back seat of the Bentley. He kept glancing in the read-view mirror at me.

"There's something different about you, Miss Danes, but I can't put my finger on it."

"What kind of different? My hair is the same."

"It's your face. I don't think you've stopped smiling since the day Ellen went to the Halloween party last week."

"Is the frequency of my smile important enough to be noticed?" Attempting to dodge his real question, I looked out the window.

"Ever since, you and Mr. Roth seem pretty chummy."

"Okay, Ben, what do you want to know, huh?"

He laughed. "Did I hit a nerve? I think I already know."

"Or maybe you don't." I crossed my arms in front of me, definitely not smiling. "If you must know, we had a nice outing together, and it's not what you think. I'm not like the girls who fawn all over you."

He laughed again. "I know, Miss Danes, you got class, that's what you got. What happened? You gonna tell me, or do I gotta guess?"

"There's nothing to tell."

"Okay, you don't have to admit what I can see." He was grinning ear to ear.

"There's nothing to see, Ben."

"Whatever you say. Just so you know, I won't talk about you. I can be discreet. I'm happy for you. Can't you tell?"

I relaxed and stopped being so defensive. "I'm thrilled you're happy. Can we please drop the subject?"

"I got it, Miss Danes." He dragged his fingers across his lips like a zipper.

***

On Halloween morning, Mrs. Chambers called me into her office after breakfast and she shut the door.

"What is it, Mrs. Chambers?" I was sure something bad had happened.

"I just want you to know your secret is safe with me." She gave me a knowing smile.

"What secret?"

"Don't be coy. Why, you and Mr. Roth." She shimmied her shoulders. "He told me to keep it under my bonnet, so to speak. My lips are sealed."

"What exactly did he say?"

"No details. He told me he planned to spend more time with you. In private. Needed my help. He doesn't want any gossip."

I squirmed in my chair and was sure the warmth showed on my face.

"There's no need to be embarrassed. Mr. Roth is a fine gentleman and his motives are truly honorable."

"They are, Mrs. Chambers. I'm not used to this sort of . . . I don't know what to call it, dealings? Have any of the staff said anything?"

"If they have, it hasn't been to me directly. But rumors get started and Mr. Roth wants to make sure your integrity remains intact."

"My goodness, did he actually say that?"

"No. Just my take on it." She pursed her lips.

"I see."

"Why so down? I thought you'd be pleased."

"It's something else."

"Then what is it? Aren't you happy with Mr. Roth?"

"Yes, well, it's . . ."

"Awkward?"

"Very." I breathed with relief. "I adore Mr. Roth and respect him. I worry I'm not right for him. You know? We come from extremely different backgrounds."

"I understand. I've seen this before."

"With Mr. Roth."

"Oh no, dearie, at other households."

"How did they work out?"

"Different situations, each one. There was the son of a wealthy European Count when I was a young girl. He was sweet on me."

"You? I thought you were married to a master chef?"

"I was. This happened years before I met my husband. I was only eighteen and working as a maid."

"What happened?"

"Oh, the master of the estate was very upset about it. The son even announced to his family he intended to marry me. It was very awkward."

"It was a long time ago? Things were different then, weren't they?"

"Yes. The problem was my lack of interest in the boy. I kept telling him no, but he was determined to marry me."

"He didn't force himself on you or anything, did he?"

"He was a gentleman, but he wouldn't believe me. I finally told the countess. There was a terrible scene between the boy and his parents."

"May I ask why you said no? Was it because you didn't feel you fit in, too?"

"Sort of. I didn't love him, nor was there any attraction on my part. Money didn't matter to me."

"I feel the same about the money. What happened then?"

"They found me a position in another household. It was the only solution they said, though I hated leaving. It devastated him, though."

"You broke his heart, poor boy. My situation differs from yours."

"In that instance, yes. But it all worked out for the best. Though I almost made the same mistake you might make." Mrs. Chambers's expression changed to one of mischief.

"Like what?"

"At my next position, I met my Mr. Chambers. I was young and he older, and there were rules against the staff fraternizing."

"Oh! So, it is similar. Except Mr. Roth doesn't have those rules. How did you end up married?"

"Mr. Chambers was persistent, in a gentlemanly way. I resisted at first until he went to the master of the house and asked for permission." A satisfied smile spread across her face.

"Smart. Obviously, he got it?"

"Much to my surprise, because Mr. Chambers waited four years before he mustered the courage." She chuckled.

I laughed too. "Mr. Roth probably won't wait four years!"

"Suppose not." She grew sad for a moment. "I do miss my Mr. Chambers."

"I'm so sorry for your loss. How lonely you must be."

"I have my son, who visits on holidays. And this house keeps me very busy." Her eyes brightened and changed the subject. "So, don't you worry, dearie, about Mr. Roth. It will all work out in its time." She reached over and patted my hand.

"I care for Mr. Roth. It's not like he's asked me to marry him. I doubt he will."

"Why do you doubt it?"

"Because so much is going on. I'm not sure you know everything."

She leaned in. "I know everything. Mr. Roth has confided with me about his late wife and Ellen. A very sorry situation."

"How do you feel about all of it?"

"Very complicated situation. I didn't know Mr. Roth's father, though I've heard tell of stories. I can see where young Mr. Roth would have trouble defying his father. But, it's not for me to judge. You are the one who needs to forgive and forget in order to move on with him. Right?"

"Lots to consider."

"It is. But I am confident everything will work out. Just give it time. You know what they say."

"What?"

"Time heals all wounds. I believe it."

"Maybe. Thank you, Mrs. Chambers, for sharing your story and for listening to me. I appreciate your support and understanding."

"It's almost like the old book, you know it? Jane Eyre."

I stopped short and almost laughed. "I know the story. It's a little similar, I guess."

Complicated had turned quickly into uncomfortable. Not sure what I expected. Now two staff members had approached me about my relationship with Hugh, and one knew everything.

After an early dinner, we all dressed up in make-shift costumes for the trick-or-treating for Ellen. I had made myself a headband with black cat ears, wore a black sweater with my black slacks, and drew whiskers on my face with eyeliner. Sylvi and Mrs. Chambers dressed up as witches, wearing pointed black hats and black dresses. Mrs. Chambers carried around a straw broom. Mr. Roth came as Dracula, wearing a black cape and fake vampire teeth. Ben was dressed as a cop. He must have borrowed the outfit from a friend. It looked real, except for the plastic gun in a holster.

We each stood behind a closed door. Ellen wore her fairy costume and knocked on the doors, yelling, "Trick-or-treat!"

It was lots of fun and afterwards we all gathered in the parlor for punch and cookies. Mr. Roth provided extra alcohol to the punch for those who desired.

Ben may not talk to the others about me and Hugh, but his face practically gave it way, anyway. Every time I looked at him, he would wink or give me a knowing smile. The staff never let on they noticed.

The days following the trip to Martha's Vineyard, we had resumed our normal schedule after dinner in the library. While Sylvi took Ellen to bed, Hugh and I would be alone, stealing a few kisses before she returned for our chats together. As much as I enjoyed the brief periods of intimacy with him, I needed my friendship with Sylvi. We had worked out our differences and my trust in her had returned.

My next day off, Sylvi and Ellen went into town with Ben. The maids had the day off, too. Yet the kitchen staff busily prepared a delicious smelling meal. I wondered who it was for with so many away.

Settled in my spot in the morning room to write, Hugh came around the corner.

"There you are. What are you up to today?" He was in a cheerful mood and almost bounced on his heels.

"The usual day off stuff. My alone time and take my walk about the grounds."

"Perfect. I'll take you for a walk right before lunch. Meet you here?"

"What are you planning?" I narrowed my eyes at him.

"Oh, a surprise." He winked, turned, and strode off.

It was very difficult to concentrate on my writing, wondering what he was up to. I turned on the radio to a pianist playing Debussy's Clair de Lune. I sat back and relaxed, closed my eyes, and dozed off. The voices of a talk-show woke me and I checked my watch. Lunch time came fast. I stood to stretch my arms and legs as I gazed out the window at the garden. None of Charlie's men were there. Everything seemed so quiet.

Firm footsteps on the marble floor caused me to turn about. "If you're trying to sneak up on me, I could hear you a mile away." I laughed.

"I don't know how to tiptoe, never learned." He grinned, his hands behind his back.

"Why are you standing there? Don't I get a hug? We appear to be very alone in here." I tempted him. Longing for more than an embrace. It had been a whole day since he'd kissed me.

"If you insist, but first . . ." He brought an arm from behind and presented me with a lovely bouquet of roses. With his free arm around my waist, he drew me close.

"The flowers are beautiful." I whispered in his ear and kissed his cheek.

He pressed his face into my neck and inhaled. "You smell divine."

His lips trailed along my throat and up to my quivering lips. My body arched into him while scintillating sensations coursed through me. Kissing this man was so amazing. What on earth would it be like to make love with him? The thought nearly sent me reeling. I trusted him more each day. Time really was a healer of wounds.

"Come with me." He took my hand, guiding me out of the room and up the staircase to the third floor. Instead of turning left, he turned right.

"I thought the south wing was off limits," I asked.

"Not to me." He chuckled.

All the way to the end of the hall, the last door on the left was ajar, and he stopped. "Now close your eyes."

I giggled and closed my eyes with anticipation.

He guided me into the room, closing the door behind us.

"You can open them now."

I opened my eyes to the most glorious sight. Roses of every color filled the room in vases on nearly every surface, along with their heady scent. Light filtered through the lace covered windows, cast a soft glow reflected from the yellow floral wallpaper. At one end of the room near the windows, two Victorian settees and a wing-backed chair in floral upholstery created a sitting area similar to the one in the sewing room. A fireplace against another wall hosted a lovely fire. In the center of the room, a small dining table dressed in white linens set for two awaited.

"It's just lovely, bright, and cheerful. What is this room?"

"Come sit first." He pulled out a chair, and I sat down.

He opened a cupboard built into the wall and removed a large tray with silver domed food covers, setting it on a butler table and rolled it next to me. With a flourish, he removed the domed lids and said, "Voilà."

"Ooh, so that's what I've been smelling all morning?" I pointed to the wall. "Is that a dumbwaiter?"

"It is."

"I've read about them. The food looks and smells wonderful."

He took the napkin folded in the shape of a bird from my place setting and snapped it to release and draped it across my lap.

"Why thank you, kind sir," I said.

Next, he put one of the prepared plates on the charger in front of me, and withdrew a bottle from the standing ice bucket. "Wine, mademoiselle?"

I nodded.

He poured a half glass of white wine into each of our goblets. "I hope you like foie gras and quiche."

"I've never had French food, but have always wanted to try it. Now tell me about this room, please."

He held up his goblet. "First a toast. To the most beautiful woman I've ever had the privilege of knowing and love."

Blushing profusely, I lifted my glass to his. "And to the most handsome man I've ever known . . . and is dreamy." I still hadn't been able to say those three little words, but he didn't even flinch at my omission.

He gave me a glowing smile. "Okay now, this room. Back in the day, my grandmother designed it for her use. This was her private chamber. She might have had guests up here, special friends or family away from staff. They installed the dumbwaiter to avoid staff from disturbing her. I think she spent most of her days up here. She wasn't a happy woman."

"Why?"

"It was a marriage of convenience. I don't think she loved my grandfather. Did he feel anything for her? I don't know."

"How sad. I appreciate all you've done today." I took a bite of the foie gras on toast points. "My, this is delicious. You know you didn't have to do this."

"Dee," he leaned forward, his eyes glistening in the light, "I'm courting you. Of course, I need to do it." He smiled, took a sip of wine, and winked.

"How Victorian, and I love it."

We ate for a bit in silence. I savored every bite and the two of us gazed into each other's eyes, as if I were living out a romance novel. It was not *Jane Eyre*. She didn't have Hugh—I did.

"Why the smug look?" he said.

"Oh, I was just thinking about how this moment is more romantic than in any romance novel I've ever read."

He laughed loudly. "Really? Stupendous."

As soon as we'd finished eating, he jumped out of his chair and pulled me up into his arms, and held me close. Music from somewhere suddenly wafted through the air. Dance music.

"Where is the music coming from?"

"It's piped in from a phonograph in the first-floor music room, directly below us. I had the chef turn it on at precisely this moment."

"He knows about us?"

"Well . . . something, I imagine."

He rocked me side to side until we were dancing around the room to a Strauss waltz. I was dizzy from the wine, the dancing, the food, and especially Hugh.

"You are sweeping me off my feet."

"That's the plan." He nuzzled my ear.

"I lov . . . I'm loving this."

He grinned and swung me around the room one more time.

He ended it with the most wonderful loving embrace and a deep, passionate kiss. I wanted more but knew it wouldn't happen there or anytime soon.

We left the room and went down the stairs to the library to wait for Sylvi and Ellen to return. It was all I could do to control myself, and Hugh appeared to have the same problem. We sat across from each other just simply staring at each other. Me with a magazine on my lap, upside down, and he with an unlit cigarette hanging from his hand.

"What are you thinking about?" He broke the silence and my gaze.

"I've been so concerned about everyone finding out about us. I know Ben, Mrs. Chambers, the chef, and perhaps Sylvi, know or have guessed."

"Probably more than we suspect. It's not time to go public yet."

"No, it's not."

"I'm working on those things I need to handle."

"Yes." My mood changed when he reminded me. I wanted to be lost in the fantasy, to forget all the secrets and lies Hugh still hadn't dealt with.

"Don't be sad, Dee. I promised to work it out. Can you be patient?"

"I'm trying. Today was very special. I'll never forget it."

The library door opened and in ran Ellen. "Miss Danes, Uncle Hugh, we had so much fun today." The bubble was burst, forcing me to land back on earth.

CHAPTER SIXTEEN

A few days before Thanksgiving, Sylvi's husband, Jack Clayton, would arrive and Hugh changed the morning breakfast schedule. We would permanently use the Breakfast Room on the main floor for the family meals. He would no longer have breakfast alone. His effort to show a more open side of himself warmed my heart. Maybe he was getting ready to tell Ellen the truth. I hoped so.

When I entered the room, everyone but Hugh had arrived. The fireplace was roaring, making it warm and inviting.

"Miss Danes," Sylvi said, "I'd like you to meet my husband, Jack Clayton."

"I've heard so much about you," I said.

He took my extended hand, shaking it robustly. "Yes, I've heard so many wonderful things about you, too," he said, his dark mustache quivering with enthusiasm. A good-looking man in his early forties with a touch of gray at the temples.

Hugh walked in just in time to join in the introductions. He and Jack had met the night before, after I retired. They resumed a conversation from earlier.

Breakfast was buffet style, but the selections were a step up from what they usually served downstairs. A server brought in freshly made coffee and poured the steaming beverage at our place settings.

"Ellen, do you want me to make a plate for you?" Sylvi asked.

"I'm old enough now, aren't I?" She looked at Sylvi and at Hugh.

"You certainly are, but you are a bit short. Here, let me lift you up." Hugh picked up Ellen so she could reach the chafing dishes without burning herself.

"I'll help." I was already at the buffet and held out a plate for Ellen.

It was an unexpected moment between the three of us, as if we were a family unit. I glanced at Hugh and he winked at me. There was something going on with him.

***

For the past two weeks, all I heard from everyone was the upcoming Pilgrim Progress reenactment in Plymouth on Thanksgiving Day. The whole town would be there, come rain or shine. When I found out we must wear Pilgrim attire, I panicked at not having something to wear. Sylvi was in the same boat. Leave it to Mrs. Chambers to come to the rescue producing costumes from storage, including one for Sylvi's husband. Ellen's costume from last year still fit and Hugh came down the stairs looking just like Captain Miles Standish.

"Don't you look smashing," he said to me, speaking in his former accent.

I laughed and curtsied. "We do, kind sir."

"I'm just glad I don't have to be part of the procession. A resident of Plymouth represents each one of the original fifty-one Pilgrims."

"I've read about it, but seeing it in person should really be something," I said.

"It's fun," Ellen said, spinning around in her little Pilgrim dress and bonnet.

"Where's the rest of the staff?" I grabbed Ellen to slow her down.

"It's a holiday," he said. "Those who live in town spend time with their families. The kitchen staff will be here just for the dinner this evening."

"Is it usual for such a large household?" I asked.

"It's usual for me. I try to allow the staff time with their families during holidays or give them time off. Tomorrow we will be on our own for meals, but the foods is there, just need to heat it up."

"Sounds good to me. Is Ben driving us?"

"He should have the limo out front."

Sylvi and Jack had just descended the staircase in their costumes, and we all piled into the limo. Ben had installed the extra seat, which Ellen and I took. Hugh, Sylvi, and Jack took the back seat.

They locked the estate up good and tight and we were off. Ben parked the limo on a side street. It looked like everyone living in the area crowded Main Street.

"Where does it begin?" Jack asked.

Hugh explained. "The procession begins at the Mayflower Society House, then moves down Water Street past Plymouth Rock, and up Leyden Street to Town Square and would end at Burial Hill. A short Pilgrim worship service takes place at the site of the original Meetinghouse."

"I've been here since August and still haven't seen Plymouth Rock," I said.

"You'll see it today." He smiled, patting my hand.

Hugh appeared to be oblivious to anyone outside of our little circle. His focus was on Ellen and me, taking the time to explain things as we passed by on foot and keeping Ellen close. I was glad he was protective. It comforted me, but I wondered if I was imagining the stares because of my insecurities.

I looked around for Becky. She was there at a distance from us, but wearing sunglasses and a scarf and not in costume. The sun wasn't particularly bright, so I thought it odd. I waved to catch her attention. She turned away and disappeared into the crowd. Perhaps she didn't want to interfere. Hugh pulled me into the rest of the group and, for that moment, I forgot about Becky.

Sylvi and Jack huddled together like newlyweds, since they had been apart for months. With Jack here, I noticed Sylvi paid less attention to Ellen, almost as if she expected me to step in. With Hugh there, we were a threesome to their twosome. We were a natural grouping, and I embraced it.

We all reached the end of the Progress at the top of Burial Hill. Just as Hugh said, a Pilgrim service began reciting a faithful recreation of the original service, and the singing of Psalms. When it was over, we walked around the town. Hugh greeted those he knew, and they reacted normally without reservation.

Ben drove us back to Rothmorton for a traditional Thanksgiving dinner in the afternoon so the staff could have their celebrations afterward. Later in the evening, we retired to the library for libation and watched some television.

Ellen had fallen asleep on Hugh's lap before the show ended. Jack scooped her up in his arms and he and Sylvi took her up. I wasn't expecting Sylvi to return for our chat, what with her husband here, and I was glad.

"Alone at last." I moved to the sofa next to him.

Hugh reached for me and held me close, kissing my neck. "Oh, and how about this?" His lips trailed down my temple, capturing my mouth, devouring it as if he hadn't seen me in weeks.

"It's becoming a habit." My hands wrapped around his neck. "And I like it."

CHAPTER SEVENTEEN

December came, and the household was busy with decorating the entire mansion. They hired additional staff during the month to help with the holidays. Hugh planned to hold the first ever New Year's Eve Party.

I had told Becky about the temporary staff hiring, but she didn't apply. It would have been nice to have a friend around, even temporarily.

Invitations were mailed and extra cleaning was done, as it was for Ellen's birthday party.

Evergreen boughs wrapped around the staircase and wreaths with big red bows hung on doors filled the air with fresh pine scent. More wreaths on all the second-floor bedroom doors, and guest rooms too, for those who need to stay over. An enormous tree sat in the middle of the parlor, so tall, it nearly touched the high ceiling, forcing the staff to stand on ladders to drape the tree in lights and ornaments at the top. Hugh directed them to leave the lower branches for Ellen to hang ornaments when we held our own tree trimming party. I loved his overblown enthusiasm to make each holiday perfect for Ellen.

***

One sleepless night, I threw on my robe and slippers and headed to the kitchen for warm milk. The hallway glowed softly from the sconces, and the guard outside Ellen's door turned to me and waved. I nodded and tiptoed down the backstairs.

When I reached the first-floor landing, there were noises coming from the direction of the morning room. I probably shouldn't have investigated on my own, but my curiosity won over logic. Plus, Hugh had ordered the guard upstairs not to leave Ellen's room. As I grew closer, it sounded like something was being ripped.

Oh God, I thought, searching for the light switch, but couldn't find it. Moonlight shone through the huge windows, making it bright enough for me to see a figure in a hooded winter coat standing in front of Ellen's portrait. When I saw the knife in an outstretched hand, I gasped. The figure turned sharply toward me and a familiar face glowered.

"Becky?" I said. "What are you doing here?"

She turned and ran out the back door into the garden, turning right along the backside of the mansion—the knife still in her hand. I started after her, catching a glimpse of the portrait. She had slashed it to shreds. I bit my lip in horror. What in the hell?

"Help!" I cried. "Stop!"

Figuring Becky would go around to the front of the mansion, I ran into the foyer, yelling for help. I reached the front door and fumbled with all the added locks. When I finally swung it open, Becky was there. She stopped at the circular drive, wildly swinging the knife in the air, looking around her as if she didn't know which way to turn.

Into the freezing cold, I went down the front steps slowly and toward the fountain, pulling my robe tighter around me. She was on the other side when she saw me.

"Don't come any closer," Becky waved the knife and stepping toward me.

"I don't understand why you are here or why you're doing this, but I'm your friend. Please put down the knife. I won't hurt you, I promise." Despite the fear rising in me, I moved closer. How did Becky get on the property and why did she damage Ellen's portrait? What was going on with her?

Becky lunged the knife at me and, though only a few yards between us, my reflex was to jump backward. I stumbled and fell.

"Dee!" Hugh shouted, running out the front door, his robe untied and flapping in the wind that suddenly whipped up.

Still on the ground, I turned toward Hugh.

Becky reached me, grabbing me around my shoulders. I tried to yank myself free, but she was too strong. She held the knife at my neck so tight the pressure of her hand on my throat caused me to choke. I pulled on her arm enough to breathe.

"Don't come any closer, or I'll slice her." Becky's voice screeched.

"Are you alright?" He said to me, stopping a few feet away.

I gave a tiny nod.

Hugh held out his hands to Becky. "I don't know you, but there is no reason to hurt an innocent person. Let Miss Danes free and you and I can talk."

Mrs. Chambers stood at the doorway, her face frozen in shock, then she went back inside. The outdoor lights came on, flooding the drive in brightness.

Becky jerked from the light and tightened her gripped. I choked again and shivered from fear and the cold. Hugh's eyes moved up, looking over Becky's head. She grunted. The knife dropped from her hand and her body fell away from me. I turned around. The guard was pulling a limp Becky a few feet from me. He must have knocked her out with the butt of his pistol. Hugh helped me stand, and I clung to him for support. We moved to the fountain.

As soon as the guard had her handcuffed, Becky roused. "Let me go. Let me go," she screamed, struggling against the guard's tight hold.

"Enough!" the guard shouted. He lifted her and dragged her to the other side of the fountain, pushing her down on the edge.

I pressed against Hugh, his arms shrouded me with his strength. I'd never been afraid for my life as I was in Becky's clutches. My knees buckled.

"I've got you," he whispered in my ear. "Here, sit down."

I sat on the edge of the fountain. Glad Becky was on the other side and secured.

Ben appeared from the garage courtyard, running as fast as he could, deterred by his limp. "What's going on? Becky? What are you doing out here?" He turned to Hugh. "Why is she in handcuffs?"

"You know this woman?" Hugh threw a surprised look at Ben.

"Uh—yeah. She's my girlfriend. I came out looking for her."

"I'll deal with you later." Hugh spoke with controlled anger, casting Ben a look of disgust.

"Becky is a waitress at the café in town," I offered. "I want to know why she vandalized Ellen's portrait, and God knows what else."

"She did what to the portrait?" Hugh said and turned to the woman. "Who are you, and why are you here?"

The guard gave Becky a nudge with his knee and tightened his grip on her arms. "You better speak up."

"Ow, that hurts. Okay, okay. I'm Rebecca Slade."

Hugh walked over to her, scrutinizing her face. "I don't know you. Are you the one who killed Ellen's cat and cut my brakes? Are you crazy?"

Becky stared back at him with a bizarre expression. "My husband thought so and the reason he locked me up in the same asylum as your wife."

"You knew Nora?" Hugh stepped back as if he'd been hit.

"I didn't need to. When I heard the rumors around the hospital about your precious Nora being pregnant, I knew. I knew." Her face twisted into a snarl and she struggled to be free of the guard, but his grip held fast.

"What did you know?"

"I knew the baby was my husband's. I asked around and a patient saw him and your wife together."

"Your husband? How was it even possible? The asylum was secure."

"Not to Herbert. When he wanted someone, he had his ways, and he got to her alright. I know. No woman could stop him. It's what drove me crazy. But I had my revenge all planned out. It took years proving I was 'normal' and released from that awful place. Ha!" Her laughter screeched, and the sound reverberated around the fountain.

"They released you? When?"

"I don't remember. A while ago. It doesn't matter when 'cause it worked. When Herbert took me home, I confronted him about Nora and the baby. He didn't care that I knew. He bragged about taking Nora. And take her, he did. He forced me down and spewed all the sordid details in my face. He could get any woman to sleep with him. I could have killed him right then and there. But I knew I had to be smart about it."

Hugh looked shaken, taking a seat next to me. My heart wrenched for him to hear such a detestable story of what had happened to Nora. The entire scene was like out of a movie.

Becky made a wicked laugh. "It was so easy. Herbert wasn't afraid of anything, least of all me. Once he was dead, I had to find out where the baby was."

"You killed your husband? My God, Becky. What kind of person are you?" I shuddered, pulling my robe tighter around me, and leaned against Hugh, grabbing his arm. His hand covered mine, giving it a tight squeeze. How could I think someone like her was a friend?

"He deserved it, didn't he?" She leered at us. "I knew Nora's name, and it didn't take long to find the Roth Estates. When I came to Plymouth and asked around, I met Ben right away. Cute, willing Ben. So easy." She laughed at Ben and turned to Hugh. "You told everyone Ellen was a cousin, but I knew the moment I saw her. She looks like Herbert. Just as cute as he was handsome. But she has to go."

"Why Ellen? Why me?" Hugh said.

"It was all your fault. Don't you see?" Her eyes blazed in fury. "If you hadn't brought Nora to the asylum, Herbert wouldn't have gone after her, and none of this would have happened." She pulled at the cuffs like a caged animal.

"You are utterly mad!" Hugh spat.

Becky shrieked hysterically, pointing to the house. "Ellen is an abomination. The issue of my evil husband and your demented wife."

"How dare you talk about Ellen and Nora. You have no right and know nothing about them. Your husband took advantage of my wife, but the child doesn't deserve your revenge." Hugh shouted this time, his body tensed against me.

Suddenly, I put everything together. "You!" I found my voice and shrieked. "How could you steal Ellen's adrenaline for her inhaler? She could have died?"

"Oh, that was easy." She shrugged. "Nursy didn't lock her doors. Ellen got off lucky. I wanted her to die."

Hugh stood up, and I thought he was going to lunge for her. But he checked himself. "You are a lunatic! You will get what's coming to you for everything."

I tried to pull him down, but he was rigid with anger.

"It hasn't been easy," Becky leered. "You had her well-guarded after that, and the staff were afraid to bring guests to the estate, even Ben. I really had to work on him until he would bring me back. I had to lie low."

Hugh turned to Ben, who had hunched over in shame. "How Ben?"

"She manipulated me. Did you hear? She admitted it. I trusted her. I didn't know."

"Tell me how, right now." Hugh left me and went for him. Ben shrank back.

I thought Hugh would hit him, but he didn't. He grabbed Ben and shook him hard. "How?"

Ben's eyes grew huge with fear. "I slipped her onto the estate and hid her in my room. How was I to know she was nuts? She must have took my keys while I slept and got in the mansion. I'm so sorry, Mr. Roth."

The sound of police sirens pierced the air.

"Go open the gate, Ben." Hugh's face was like stone.

Ben retreated inside and soon the police came down the drive with lights flashing.

Hugh turned back to me. "Dee, your neck, it's bleeding. Go inside and have Mrs. Chambers or Sylvi clean it up and sit in front of a fire. You're frozen. I'll be in later."

"I'm fine, really." I lied. My hands shook as I took a handkerchief from the pocket of my robe and pressed it to my neck.

"Please." His eyes pleaded, full of worry.

I nodded and went into the house, having heard enough from Becky. My stomach turning over from fear and disgust. It was Ellen that worried me, hoping she hadn't awakened. I headed for the staircase and saw Ben sitting on the first step with his head in his hands and Sylvi leaning over the railing several steps up.

"What's going on? Why were you outside?" Sylvi said as she descended. "I heard the sirens. Don't worry, I checked on Ellen and she's sleeping like a rock."

"What a relief. Let's go to the library. You will not believe this, and I need a good stiff drink."

Sylvi's eyes nearly popped. Since I rarely drank hard liquor.

In the library, Mrs. Chambers was busy stoking a fire in the grate when she heard us. "Miss Danes, your neck."

"Good grief, I just noticed." Sylvi said. "Are you alright?"

"Yes, Sylvi, could you give me a hand with it?"

"Of course. Let me get my medical bag." She hurried from the room.

"Can I get you anything?" Mrs. Chambers said.

"A brandy, please." I collapsed on the sofa while she poured the drink. I took the glass and sipped it at first. The warmth relaxed my muscles, and I took another sip. I was shivering.

"You must be chilled to the bone, dearie. Here . . ." She wrapped one of the thick lap blankets around me and I managed a wan smile.

Sylvi returned with her bag in record time and I filled her in on as much as I understood about Becky while she attended my wound.

"What an incredible story." Sylvi said while applying a bandage.

"The whole incident was beyond belief. Becky is a lunatic, and I never noticed. I thought she was a friend. All the time, she was using me for information."

"She must be quite an actress," Mrs. Chambers said. "And Ben said she was his girlfriend? I never even suspected he had one, or wanted one. Such a flighty one he is."

"Apparently, Becky had poured all her hatred and resentment of what her husband had done on Ellen. I suppose in her mind the child represented the adulterous evil of her husband's pursuit of Nora." I leaned back into the sofa.

"Do you think Becky would have really hurt you?" Sylvi closed her bag and sat next to me.

"Yes, if she thought it would help somehow. I'm just glad this is all over. The threats, the vandalism, the attempts on Hugh's life, and violence from Becky."

"No kidding," Sylvi said.

"I hear voices in the foyer." Mrs. Chambers went to the door when it opened.

Hugh entered, followed by the inspector.

"Dee, the inspector needs to take your statement."

The inspector excused Sylvi, since she witnessed nothing, and she went back upstairs to check on Ellen. The rest of the night was a blur, and I was exhausted by the time the police left. Hugh put his arm around me to escort me to my room. I let him inside and shut the door.

"It's over and you're safe now." He slid his hands around my waist. "We all are safe. I thought I might lose you." He breathed into my hair, kissing my neck, then my lips.

I held onto him with all my might. "Would you sit with me awhile? I'm not ready to be alone."

Without a word, he took me to my bed, removed my robe and slippers and tucked me in, pulling the covers up under my chin. He kissed my forehead and sat in the chair near the bed. I reached for him and he took my hand, holding it until I fell asleep.

CHAPTER EIGHTEEN

Hugh had left by the time I awakened. It was so late in the morning I missed breakfast, needing coffee badly. There was a note on the night table from him saying he would make excuses for me and have Sylvi spend the day with Ellen. He signed it, "Yours, H."

After I showered and dressed, my mood improved some, and I headed downstairs to the kitchen. I begged the chef for a cup of coffee and took a seat in the staff dining area. The previous night's events swirling in my head. One thing was certain, with Becky in custody, the air seemed clearer and I breathed easier.

"Ah, there you are," Mrs. Chambers's cheerful voice was much welcomed. "Why didn't you use the intercom? I'd have sent breakfast up to you."

"Wasn't hungry. My gosh, it's nearly lunchtime, isn't it? Did you get any sleep?"

"I don't need much sleep, dearie. I'm fine," she said. "You take your time. I think Mr. Roth is in the library in a meeting." She gave me a knowing look, and I realized there were no more secrets among our elite group after last night.

The chef brought me a plate of toast and jam along with the coffee, and I took my time as Mrs. Chambers suggested. I wondered if Hugh was meeting with the police.

When I finished, I went up to the first floor. As I reached the library, Hugh's voice bellowed from inside. I stopped to listen.

"You purposely put Ellen in danger by blatantly breaking the rules about unauthorized persons on the estate grounds. Not to mention the rule about having women in your room overnight. How and why did you do it?"

Ben's voice was much lower, but I made it out.

"I hid her in the trunk."

"Unbelievable! What were you thinking, man?"

"I'm in love with her. Love's blind, ya know."

"This is serious. Your jokes are not funny. I don't know what to do with you."

"I'm seriously in love."

"With a lunatic! Ben, come to your senses. It's over, understand?"

There was a silent pause.

"Mr. Roth, I know I don't deserve no more favors. You done right by me, giving me this job and all. I broke your trust. If you want me outta here, I understand."

"Exactly right. You've broken my trust. I'm doing my damnedest to keep it under wraps. As far as I know, the staff doesn't know about your involvement, except Mrs. Chambers, Miss Danes, and Nurse Clayton, who I've sworn to secrecy. I expect the same from you until I decide whether you stay or go."

"Thanks, Mr. Roth. I'll try to make it up to you."

"Now go. I'll let you know as soon as I've decided."

When the library door opened, I stepped away from the door and tried to look like I was just reaching it.

"Sorry, Miss Danes. Didn't know you were there."

"It's okay. I didn't know anyone was in the library."

"Mr. Roth is still in there, if you need to speak to him." Ben averted his eyes, his shoulders slumped.

"Actually, I'd like to talk to you, if you don't mind . . . about Becky."

"Sure thing, anytime, like now?"

I hoped he didn't think I judged him. He made a terrible mistake for love.

"Let me get my coat. I'll meet you in the garage."

He nodded as he slouched, appearing smaller than usual. He was in love with someone who had deceived him. Something I was experiencing myself. If anyone could understand what I was going through, it might be Ben and he would need my understanding as well.

I retrieved my coat from my room and went out of the service entrance into the courtyard. The cold wind cut against my face and I put on my gloves. I thought about the night before, shivering in my nightgown and robe with Becky's knife at my throat, and shuddered.

Banging noises came from inside the garage as I walked towards the open bay door. He was in the back, slamming a large hammer onto an empty anvil.

"You trying to reshape the anvil?" My attempt to lighten the mood fell flat.

Ben looked up and put the hammer down. "Caught me letting out my anger. Better on the anvil than on some person."

"Like Becky?"

"Oh gee, no Miss Danes. I wouldn't hurt a woman. Just the world, ya know. Ya think you know who to trust and then . . . bam!"

"I know exactly what you mean." I moved closer to him and looked around for somewhere to sit.

"Sorry. Not really a good place for serving up tea." He snorted.

I leaned against a car, grateful he kept them clean. "I'm fine. You probably feel pretty bad about the Becky situation, though."

"Yep. Don't know if Mr. Roth will let me stay on after what I did. Breaking the rules and all the trouble Becky caused and might have caused if you hadn't found her last night. Plain nuts what she did to Ellen's painting. Glad she didn't hurt you any. You, okay?"

My hand went to the bandage on my neck. "It was pretty scary. She had really lost it and I wasn't sure what would happen."

"So, what d'ya wanna know about her?" His brow crinkled.

"She befriended me too, in town, and at first, I thought she was nosy, then I was grateful to find a friend outside of Rothmorton. Were there any signs of what she was up to?"

"Nothin'. Must be what happened to me. Guess you think a guy like me wouldn't be lonely. She saw it. And used it against me. I fell in love with her. She had this way of explainin' things. I believed everything she said."

"Like what?" I found it hard to think of him being in love with someone. He seemed like he didn't really need people. Boy, was I wrong.

"One night I woke up, and she was coming in from outside, which was strange 'cause we fell asleep together, ya know. I asked her where she went, and she says she needed a smoke and didn't want to disturb me. Didn't think nothin' of it. When it came out, she was the one doin' all those terrible things. Made me feel like a real dummy, ya know."

"Well, if you are, so am I. She was a master at manipulation and deceit. She murdered her husband and tried to kill Mr. Roth and me. You and I are both lucky we are alive, I guess."

"She got me to tell her things I shouldn't have." He looked down at his feet and kicked over an empty can.

"What did you tell her?"

"About me driving you and Mr. Roth to Boston. Then she slashed the tires and left the threatening note? It's all my fault."

"Did you tell Mr. Roth this?"

"Yeah. He should have been madder at me than he was."

"What about the brakes?"

"None of it would have happened if I hadn't snuck her in here. She seemed so interested in cars. She asked me questions about engines and stuff. I even showed her things."

"How could you have known, Ben? I feel deceived too. I thought Becky was a friend."

"I thought you and her were getting chummy. I was afraid she'd tell 'bout me. Shoulda put it together, the brakes, and her interest. But I didn't know who she really was. I still don't understand exactly what her connection is."

"No one did. You didn't hear anything she said before you came outside last night?"

"Naw. I was shocked to see her cuffed."

"You didn't know about Mrs. Roth?"

"I heard rumors she'd been in a mental hospital. Didn't make sense to me."

"Really?" Mrs. Chambers said they could not control what people gossiped about in town. Maybe someone working at the estate at the time knew and told someone in town. "No point in worrying about it all now. Have the police questioned you?"

"Oh boy, sure did. I'm worried they'd call me in during the trial."

"Will there be a trial?"

"I don't really know. Just assumed."

"They have not charged you with anything like being an accomplice?"

"They said I didn't have no motive. Believed everything I said. I think."

"Good. I should probably let you get back to work."

"Hey, what d'ya think Becky did to her husband? I mean, how she killed him?"

"I shudder to think. Don't know or want to know."

"Yeah, but it makes ya think. Just being around someone like her. I feel dirty all over 'cause of her. Bein' with her and stuff."

"Give it time, you'll get over it."

"Yeah. Thanks for listening. It's not like I have anyone to talk to about it."

I returned to the house and found Hugh waiting by the back door.

"Let me take your coat," he said with a calm expression.

"Why are you down here?"

"I heard you outside the library door and was curious. What did you want to talk to Ben about?"

I walked past him, looking around the kitchen for the staff. It was empty. Hugh followed me with my coat to the library. The door was open. He draped my coat over a chair and I removed my gloves and warmed my hands at the fire.

"Well?" he said.

"It was nothing. I certainly hope you've given up your suspicions of Ben and me?"

He gave a guilty look.

"Now really." I let out a frustrated huff. "Ben and I were both duped by Becky. I thought we could commiserate. What did you think we were doing?"

He held his hands up in defense. "I'm sorry. My emotions are a mess. Did you get any information I couldn't?"

"Might have. Do you blame him for what Becky did?"

"Not entirely."

I pointed to the portable bar. "Do you mind? My nerves are still a mess, too."

He raised his eyebrows. "It's not even noon, you sure?"

I nodded. "Can't get last night out of my head. I'm still pretty shaken. Don't worry, this won't become a habit."

"I'll get it, brandy?"

"A little." I took a seat on the sofa and leaned back, resting my head, staring at the high ceiling, noticing for the first time its intricately carved wood panels.

He poured two and handed me one, then sat down next to me. "You haven't told me about your friendship with Becky. How do you know her?"

I took the brandy like a shot, letting it warm my empty stomach. Its effect took over. "Met her at the café in town. She was friendly. I had no reason to suspect her of anything other than being another single woman looking for friendship."

"Of course." His hand rested lightly on my shoulder, and I put my hand over his. It was comforting.

"Becky was the one who told me you had been married."

"Mrs. Chambers didn't tell you about my irrational rules?" He half laughed.

"Oh, so you realize it was strange." I smirked. "No, she forgot to give me the warning. I thought you were single. I didn't question her motives. Instead, I was curious why you made the rule."

"It's all over now. For us at least."

"I'm worried about Ben. He mentioned he might be called in during Becky's trial."

"If there is one."

"No trial?"

"It's all out," he said. "The newspapers have the story, well, a story, I should say. I spent all morning working it out with the police commissioner. The papers only say there was a break-in here and an arrest."

"What's happening with Becky?"

Hugh swirled the untouched brandy in his glass. "The inspector told me they have a signed confession from her and because the murder of her husband occurred in another jurisdiction, they will extradite her."

"That's a relief. The farther away she is will make me feel all the safer."

"But . . . I assume she still has some smarts left and will hire a lawyer who will try to get her off on an insanity plea. She's nuts for sure, but that won't get her off the charge for murder."

"Won't it all get into the papers about what she did here, too?"

"If I press charges, probably."

"If?"

"The murder happened before she came here and is a more serious offense. If and when she will be convicted and sentenced, whether to prison or an institution for the criminally insane, I may not need to do anything. We'll cross that bridge when we come to it."

He stood and went to the window to gaze out. His thoughts must have wandered, for he grew quiet.

"What about what you did?" I wanted to bring him back to our conversation.

"Me? Oh, you mean about keeping Nora's death a secret? It'll come out, I'm afraid. My lawyers tell me not releasing the information to Nora's family or anyone else about her death isn't a crime, just not very considerate. The attending physician completed the death certificate accurately, and the funeral home processed everything in secret but within the laws. Sylvia has agreed not to prosecute for not being informed when Nora died."

"Glad to hear. By the way, I found Nora's grave."

"You've been to the Rothmorton Cemetery?"

"Discovered it by accident while riding my bicycle one day. I wish you had told me, though."

"One of the many things I should have done. I'm sorry." He took the brandy in one swallow.

"Just disconcerting. I dislike cemeteries. Does Sylvi know?"

"Yes, I took her out there after you went to Illinois when I told her the rest of the story."

"So, Nora had a kind of funeral. How did you keep it a secret from the staff?"

"In the dead of night, just like in the movies."

"Don't joke."

"Sorry, it's not a joke. We did it at night."

"When you tell Ellen the truth, will you take her to the grave?"

"Eventually. If she wants to go. All in the future, Dee."

"By the way, what will you do about Ellen's damaged portrait?"

"It's being taken to Mr. Greene's studio in Boston. He'll paint a new one just like it. I didn't tell him how it happened and he didn't ask."

"That's wonderful. Such a sad story. The press, not to mention your friends and business associates, will ask a lot of questions not shared in the story. How will you handle it?"

"I'll handle it. Don't worry."

How could I not worry? Ellen could find out from outside sources. Even though Hugh said the entire story wouldn't get out. There was no guarantee and he couldn't keep her cooped up at Rothmorton forever. He needed to address it with Ellen. I struggled with his procrastination. Or was it a weakness? I couldn't tell which.

"How do you feel about what Becky told us?"

He shrugged his shoulders. "Like what?"

"About Nora and Becky's husband."

"Oh, I see what you mean." He sat back down next to me, his face looking suddenly older. He wiped his hands across his face as if to clear his mind. "I feel sad and responsible. She shouldn't have been left at the asylum for so long."

"You weren't responsible for what happened to her. You thought she was in a safe place."

"I did, and look what happened."

"It was a terrible thing, but you couldn't have predicted it."

"You're right . . . When I found out she was pregnant, my first thought was rape. Nora refused to say. Now it's confirmed, I feel sick to my stomach. I want to punch that guy for what he did. Becky made it impossible for me to take my revenge."

"I don't blame you. No one should get away with such a horrid crime. But revenge drove Becky to what she did to us. What did it accomplish? Thankfully, none of us were hurt by her hands."

Hugh looked at me with pain-filled eyes and took my hand. "Right again. You are my rock, Dee. I need your steady head to keep me focused on the upside of things. I just hope Becky pays for what she's done."

"I choose to believe justice will prevail. And I think Nora was trying to protect you from knowing the truth."

"My God, what she went through . . . the war, her mind, the rape, then dying." His voice broke, and he hung his head, his shoulders shook.

It took all my strength not to cry, too. My arms held him as he sobbed. His healing had begun, and we bonded in a way I never thought we would.

***

Ben got to keep his job with the understanding if he broke one more rule, he was out. I thought Hugh very generous, considering. He said if others could forgive him for his transgressions, he could forgive Ben, and that's true.

My biggest concern, and of course Hugh's too, was how to keep everything from Ellen. The morning the story about the break-in hit the papers, and the phone was ringing off the hook.

I was early for breakfast, finding the first-floor breakfast room empty, so I went downstairs. Mrs. Chambers had just hung up the phone in her office as I passed by. She threw her hands in the air. "I can't take this any longer. Is Mr. Roth in the library?"

I shrugged ignorance just as Hugh walked in.

"I'll take the rest of the calls, have them redirected to the library. You can have the rest of the day off."

"Thank you, Mr. Roth. It's my day off, anyway." Mrs. Chambers put on her coat, grabbed her purse, and left.

"It's worse than you thought." I turned to Hugh.

"Okay, I was wrong," he said. The phone rang again, and he answered. "Speaking . . . no comment." He slammed the receiver.

"That's one way of handling it." I rolled my eyes.

CHAPTER NINETEEN

On Christmas Eve, we had a sumptuous dinner retiring afterward to the parlor to help Ellen trim the tree.

"Uncle Hugh, can I hang this one?" Ellen held up a rather large blown glass ornament with a tiny sleigh inside.

"Of course, just be careful. Remember, it's an old family heirloom." He did an aside with his hand to me. "Hand-blown in Germany and brought here by my grandmother."

The sound of breaking glass made us all turn to find Ellen looking in horror at the floor where the ornament lay in a million pieces.

"I'm sorry!" She cried, with tears streaming down her cheeks.

Hugh's face was in shock, but only for a second as he rushed to Ellen's side. "There, there now, Ellen, it's just a thing, it's of no matter. Please don't cry." He brushed her tears away with gentle fingers and hugged her tight.

"I didn't mean to drop it," she said.

"It's all right." He patted her back. "Accidents happen."

He surprised me, especially after he bragged about the ornament. Ellen truly was more important to him and anything, maybe even me.

Right on cue, Mrs. Chambers appeared with a dustpan and broom and quickly swept up the glass. "Don't cry, dearie," she said to Ellen. "It's all cleaned up now, see?"

"Let's look for another one," I said, looking in the ornament box for something smaller for her to handle. I held up some metallic painted pine cones in red and green. They were glass, but more substantial than the broken one. "How about these?"

"Perfect, Miss Danes," Sylvi said, taking one and putting a hook on it.

I held the other one out for Ellen, waiting for her to come around.

Hugh released Ellen and stepped back. "Go on." He said in a cheerful tone.

"Okay," she sniffled, taking the green ornament from my hand. She let her uncle guide it to a place on the tree.

Ellen recovered quickly, taking ornaments from each of us to hang on the tree. A server entered, carrying a tray of hot chocolate. We all relaxed and Hugh whispered something to the server who left the room. Minutes later, Christmas music wafted through the air, setting the mood.

With the rest of the ornaments hung on the tree, Ellen grew drowsy and fell asleep, snuggled up to Hugh. He took her to bed. Sylvi and I put our few packages under the tree, and then she and Jack went upstairs. When Hugh returned, he motioned for me to stay, so I poured myself a drink from the bar and gazed at the tree. A warm, comforting feeling filled me.

He took my hand and guided me to the settee. His face beamed. Did he have another secret to tell me? Then, low and behold, he got down on one knee and drew something from his pocket. It couldn't be. He opened a tiny box and the sparkle from an extraordinarily large sapphire ring made me gasp.

"I . . . this is so unexpected."

"I am so much in love with you, I can barely speak in your presence. You take my breath away and I would be extremely honored if you would be my wife."

His gaze was loving and hopeful, and I should have been deliriously happy, but I was truly speechless.

An awkward silence sat like lead between us. I didn't know what to say. What could I say? Was I in love with him? Yes. Did I trust him? If I didn't before, I did now. Then why was I hesitating?

"Dee?"

"I want to say yes . . ."

"Then . . ."

This was the moment I had dreamed of my whole life. A handsome man, and a wealthy man, was waiting for my answer and all I could think of was whether I belonged? I wanted to belong. My silly insecurities and self-doubts were still standing in my way.

I stood and took a few steps away from him and he rose, his face completely deflated. My heart lurched. I didn't want to hurt him. "I love you."

"Well, damn, if you love me, why are you hesitating? Everything I promised is done. Except for telling Ellen and you were okay with waiting."

"You have. It's something else."

"Then what is it?"

"It's me. I don't know if I'm enough."

"Enough? You mean for me? Of course, you are. You are everything I've ever wanted in a woman, in a wife."

"I'm not like you or this world."

"Will you stop? I'm not like the others, haven't you realized? I'm evolving, changing, wanting a different life. Is it this big old mansion and the stuffy people I associate with? They are nothing to me. It's you, Dee."

"No, I'm not, it'll never work!" I ran out and up to my room, crying desperate tears.

"Dee!" Hugh's voice dimmed in the background.

***

I shut my door and locked it, then threw myself on the bed. "What is the matter with me?"

All night I laid awake going over everything he said, and my feelings for him were stronger than ever. I loved him, so what was standing in my way? Was it really about fitting in? Confusion consumed me until I couldn't see straight and fell asleep.

When the light filtered through the windows on Christmas morning, my body was shaking from lack of sleep. I dragged myself into the bathroom and peered into the mirror. Red-rimmed eyes and puffy under-eye bags glowered at me like a finger pointing at what a mess I'd made of everything. How would I face him now?

We all met in the breakfast room. Half the kitchen staff took the rest of the day off to be with their families. The other staff would switch for the following day. Hugh wanted a full dinner for all of us. I noticed Mrs. Chambers wasn't there, and I was happy for her since she had family visiting from out of town.

Ellen was eager to eat quickly, and open presents, but Hugh made her slow down. I couldn't look at him, though his eyes were on me, willing me to raise mine. I picked at my food, unable to eat. Is this what heartsick is like?

"Miss Danes, are you feeling well this morning?" Sylvi said.

"Didn't sleep much. I must look a sight."

"Not at all. You just seem lethargic, and you haven't eaten a bite. Sure you're okay?"

"I'll be fine." I glanced up at Hugh and saw his stricken face. He looked like he hadn't slept either, dark circles under his eyes. I cringed with guilt, knowing it was my fault. How could I be so selfish, worrying only about myself, running from him as if he had hit me? He had treated me with respect and love and I dashed his proposal to dust. Staring at my plate again, I swallowed hard to keep the tears at bay.

Hugh turned toward Jack and struck up a conversation until everyone had finished eating.

"Now, Uncle Hugh?"

When he nodded yes, she practically ran.

"Ellen, slow down," he said.

"Sorry."

She slowed to a snail's pace, making us all laugh.

Hugh played Santa, handing out the gifts from under the tree, one by one. Most of them went to Ellen, of course. Sylvi gave me a gift of a lovely winter knitted scarf.

"It's lovely Sylvi, I think we have the same taste," I chuckled.

When she opened my gift to her and discovered a winter scarf, we both laughed.

"You're right, Dee. I love it," Sylvi said.

Surrounded with packages, Ellen opened the wrapped gifts as quickly as possible, knowing they were from Uncle Hugh. Hugh labeled the larger unwrapped toys from Santa. A stuffed bear, as big as Ellen, was her immediate favorite. When she opened my gift to her, *The Tall Book of Fairy Tales*, she jumped up and down.

"Thank you, Miss Danes. I love fairy tales."

"I know." My mouth spread into a smile. How I wanted to be a mother to Ellen. Marrying Hugh would make all my dreams come true. If I just erased all my fears and self-doubts.

Ellen's laughter brought me back to the moment.

Sylvi gave Ellen a little toy tiara. "I can wear this with my fairy costume! Thank you, Nurse Clayton." Then she turned to Hugh. "Let me give those, please?" She pointed to two small packages still under the tree.

He handed them to her with a wink and a smile. His mood improved while enjoying Ellen and watching her with love.

Ellen gave one to me and kissed me on the cheek and then gave the other one to Sylvi, kissing her cheek, too.

"Why thank you, Ellen." I tore off the wrapping to find a beautiful sterling silver bracelet with an engraved plate with my name in script.

"Turn it over," Ellen said.

I read the engraving aloud. "To the best teacher in the world, Love, Ellen." Tears welled up, blurring my vision. "It's beautiful." I opened my arms wide, and she ran to me, throwing her arms around my neck. I kissed her cheek.

Sylvi had opened her gift to find a similar bracelet, also engraved.

"Read yours Nurse Clayton," Ellen said.

Sylvi took an emotion filled breath. Her eyes welling with tears. "To a wonderful healer, Love, Ellen." They hugged.

Hugh gave me a special look. I knew the gift was from him too and I couldn't help but return his smile. His eyes watered and looked away. What pain I had caused him, and my stomach twisted.

The next couple of days were torturous. I tried to offer my help for the New Year's Party, which was right around the corner. Mrs. Chambers wouldn't have it and told me to enjoy my time off since Ellen took a break from her studies. I spent much of the time thinking about what I had done to Hugh and avoided him, except at meals, though he had taken to eating breakfast earlier, alone. Strange, him not being with us in the mornings. I still did nothing.

Alone in my room one afternoon, there was a knock on the door.

"Dee, you in there? It's Sylvi."

I cracked open the door. "Hi."

"Can I come in?"

"Sure. I was trying for a nap, but couldn't." I sat on the edge of my bed.

Sylvi took the side chair. "Look, it's probably none of my business, but I care about you and know something is wrong. It's Hugh, isn't it?"

I slumped my shoulders, letting the tears fall freely.

"Oh, honey," Sylvi sat beside me and put her arm around my shoulders. "I hope it's not a lover's quarrel. Did this happen on Christmas Eve? The two of you have looked miserable ever since."

I nodded. "I'm such a fool to think I could ever fit in to Hugh's world."

"How can you think such a thing? The two of you are a splendid match."

I sniffled into my hanky and looked up at her. "You really think so?"

"Sure do. It's obvious he is head over heels. I've known for months how you've felt. Probably before you did."

"You're right. I've been fighting against my feelings. He's everything I've dreamed of and more, but . . ."

"What happened?"

"I'm just a simple farm girl."

"Pooh. You are nothing of the sort." She took my shoulders and gave me a gently shake. "You've got smarts, talent, and style. If you want to fit in, you will. Has he said something to set you off?"

"Well . . . sort of." I blew my nose and brush away the tears, not ready to tell her how I had rejected his proposal. "Thanks Sylvi. I think I need some time alone and to get some rest. Maybe things will look better later."

"Sure thing. I'll check in on you for dinner, okay?"

After Sylvi left, I spent hours considering everything Sylvi had said and things Mrs. Chambers had told me, but could not decide what to do. I wondered if I ever would.

CHAPTER TWENTY

Whenever Hugh and I were in the same room, the tension between us was unbearable. Most of the time, he didn't even look at me. He was all I could think about.

Three days before the party, after everyone retired, I planned to sneak to Hugh's suite on the other side of the stairs to talk to him, when I heard his door open. I hid behind a curtain in the dark hall until he descended the stairs. When he had trouble sleeping, he would go down for a second nightcap in the library. I followed him. He didn't hear me enter, and immediately poured himself a very large brandy.

"I'll have one too," I said.

Hugh wheeled around, almost dropping his glass. "I didn't hear you." He started to smile, then pulled it into a scowl and hurried to pour me a brandy. I went to the fireplace.

"It's cold in here. Thought the fire would be lit, then remembered the staff was asleep."

"I'll start it." He handed me the glass and grabbed a couple of logs from the bin.

Taking a seat in the wing-backed chair closest to the fireplace to watch him, my mind had gone blank. The words I'd heard in my mind over and over all day were no longer there, yet I wasn't nervous or even tired. Being near him had a soothing effect on me.

Once the fire roared in the grate, he warmed his hands, then turned to me with an expectant expression, waiting for me to start.

I opened my mouth. "I'm so sorry."

His eyebrows lifted, still waiting.

"Sometimes I'm my own worst enemy." I took a big gulp of the brandy for courage and coughed as it burned going down, but it helped. "I've been consumed with this belief I wasn't good enough for you and I didn't belong in your world. Old conditioning. With everything going on, it just fueled my belief. But I was wrong. I hurt you on Christmas Eve, and I'm terribly sorry. Can you forgive me?"

Hugh stepped toward me, reached into his coat pocket and withdrew the little box. Had he been carrying it around with him?

My hand went to my throat, for I was sure he had changed his mind.

He got down on his knee and put the box in my hand, wrapping both his hands around it, staring deep into my eyes. "Now tell me you don't want to be married to me."

He cupped his hands around my face, kissing my forehead, then each eyelid, then he kissed my neck, and pressed his lips to mine. I nearly swooned. "Tell me." He whispered in my ear.

"I can't tell you that. Because I love you and I desperately want to be married to you."

"Hallelujah!" He kissed me again.

"Hush," I said, "You'll wake the whole place." I kissed him back and suddenly my whole being was resolved. My reservations had evaporated.

He drew back to take the box from my hand and opened it. Taking the ring, he slid it up onto my left-hand ring finger.

"Just wanted to make sure it fits, and you'd let me." He laughed.

"Oh Hugh, it's spectacular." An enormous octagonal cut blue sapphire surrounded by diamonds in a platinum setting dazzled me.

"Belonged to my mother. I hope you don't mind."

"Mind? Are you mad? I'm so honored to wear it. She was a special person."

"Looks great on you, too."

"I love you with all my heart. Thought I'd broken mine and yours, too."

"Never." He kissed me again. "But, let's not tell anyone yet. I want to make a formal announcement at the party next week."

"Okay, except, can I tell Sylvi? I want to ask her to be my matron of honor."

"Of course. We both know she can keep a secret."

I rolled my eyes, and we chuckled over the joke.

He got up, pulling me with him to the sofa, where we became entangled in no time. The passion mounted quickly and if we hadn't been in the library, it could have gotten out of hand.

"Dee, I want you so much."

"I want you, too . . ."

"We'll wait." He took a deep breath, pulling back.

Relief ran through me, along with several other emotions. I certainly didn't want my first time to be in a moment of passion on the library sofa.

"I want it to be absolutely perfect and on our wedding night."

"Oh Hugh, it's important to me, too. When though?"

"Whenever you are ready. We can take as long as you need."

"I don't want to wait very long. Now I know for sure it's the right thing, maybe a spring wedding?"

"Whatever you want." He kissed me again, deeply, and his love filled me to the brim as warm tingles fluttered all over me. I couldn't imagine what our wedding night would be like.

***

Hugh was planning to make a surprise announcement of our engagement at the New Year's Party. Even though Becky was no longer in the Plymouth area, some of Becky's confession leaked to the press, connecting her to Hugh's former wife. Nothing about Ellen, thankfully. Yet with all the publicity, we weren't sure if anyone would actually attend.

R.S.V.P.'s had trickled in initially, if not for the unveiling, possibly out of curiosity, but the last week the numbers had raised significantly. Mostly

Hugh's business associates and their wives, not too many of the society neighbors in the Plymouth and Cape area.

Regardless, I was excited about the engagement and planning of the wedding. Neither of us wanted to wait very long, no six-month planning for us. A church wedding didn't matter to me nor to Hugh, though he wanted a formal wedding. His marriage to Nora had been a civil ceremony and rushed. He wanted something special for me, so we had the ceremony in the Rothmorton garden.

***

Two days before the party, Hugh dragged me down to the parlor, telling me he had a guest coming, especially for me.

"Darling," he said, "I know how self-conscious you are about your clothes and fitting in at parties. After our announcement, you'll never have to worry about it again, but in the meantime."

"What do you mean? I was planning to wear the blue dress. That's not good enough?"

"It's not that. I want you to be wearing the most fabulous gown of any woman at the party. Understand? It's important to me. In a few minutes, the fashion buyer from Saks Fifth Avenue in New York is coming here to fit you into one of their latest gowns."

"Today? Now?" I thought I would faint.

"It's a special favor he's doing for me, uh, us."

The doorbell rang, and Mrs. Chambers answered, escorting the guests into the parlor. I motioned for her to stay. The buyer arrived with her full entourage with gowns in special bags and even a rack, with staff fluttering around. I sat dumbfounded, watching as they created a mini fashion show for me with three models from New York City dressed in couture evening gowns designed by top designers.

I sat mesmerized, watching each model spin around, showing off the gowns just for me. Hugh sat by my side, holding my hand, thoroughly enjoying it himself.

"Now the color on this one would bring out the green in your eyes," he said. "Which one are you going to try on, Dee?"

"Oh gosh, I don't know. I love them all."

The last model was wearing a white velvet gown trimmed in gold lame, with long sleeves. The bodice fitted snugly with the skirt swooping down and flaring out at the bottom. "I love it, but how in the world would I fit into it?"

"Ah, Madame," said the assistant couturier, "you would wear a corset, of course."

I chuckled, "I thought women stopped wearing those."

The couturier frowned. "If you need something looser fitting, you would need a different designer."

"I didn't mean to offend. Actually, I would like to try it." I smiled, embarrassed, and glanced at Hugh.

He looked quite amused. "I'd love to see it on you."

Another of the assistants guided me out of the parlor and into the guest restroom, large enough to accommodate ten guests, where they set up for the fitting. Two ladies assisted me in undressing and pouring my body into the undergarments. There was a full-length mirror on the wall. The dress slid over my head and across my newly contrived figure like liquid. A perfect fit. The two ladies chattered to each other about what needed to be done. I gazed in the mirror, not recognizing myself.

"Dee," Hugh called from the other room. "Are you coming out in that thing or not?"

"Thing?" I muttered, then turned to the assistants. "You can fix this later. I want to show Mr. Roth."

"Of course, Madame." They ushered me out, lifting the too long hem.

The pumps I wore were tall enough. Despite the very snug fit of the corset, it made me feel like a million bucks. When I entered the parlor, there was a loud gasp. It was Hugh.

"The dress is perfect. We'll take it," he said to the couturier.

"Thank you, darling, I love it." I kissed his cheek.

"You'll knock 'em dead." He grinned from ear to ear.

***

The next day, I went to Sylvi's room.

"Come in," Sylvi said when I knocked.

I opened the door and found her standing in front of her mirror, wearing a new dress. "For the party?"

"Yes, what do you think? Fancy enough?" She grabbed the full skirt and swished it back and forth. "Four taffeta petticoats. Don't you love the sound?"

"Yes, and it's beautiful. Emerald green is perfect for you. Where did you get it?"

"Jack brought it from New York. Can you believe it? What a surprise. When he heard about the party, he said he still had business up there and he came back with it. He sure has great taste." Sylvi glowed.

"He's a keeper."

"Definitely! I heard about the fashion show downstairs yesterday. I was told to keep Ellen out of the way. What happened?"

I sat on the edge of her bed. "Hugh bought me a designer original for the party."

"Really? You worked things out from whatever happened on Christmas Eve?"

I nodded.

"You're not uncomfortable with him buying you an expensive dress?"

"Uh, not at all, because . . ."

Sylvi tilted her head with a quizzical expression. "Because of what?"

I stuck my hand out, letting the big rock glitter in the light. "This."

Sylvi's mouth dropped open. "You've got to be kidding. You're engaged?"

"Yes, and I want you to be my matron of honor." I giggled with glee, barely holding my excitement.

Sylvi sat on the bed next to me and gave me a hug and held my hand to look at the ring closer. "Unbelievable. But, I'm not at all surprised. I've been waiting for you to tell me about the two of you. Why haven't you?"

"To be honest, I was being pigheaded and resisting him. I had convinced myself I didn't fit into his world. My insecurities held me back."

"I'm thrilled for you. And yes, a thousand times, yes, I'll be your matron of honor. How exciting."

"Now you can't tell a soul until after the formal engagement announcement, at the New Year's Eve party."

"Not a word from me. Is it the real reason for the party?"

"He didn't propose until Christmas Eve, after the party was planned. When he first asked me, I said no."

"Ah, and the reason you looked like death on Christmas morning. Why didn't you tell me that day I dropped by?"

"I almost did, but I was in such turmoil. Thank you for being there for me. I was such a mess. You really helped."

"I did?"

"Your words of encouragement helped me come to my senses. I finally told him yes."

"I bet he was counting on you saying yes. His feelings have been plastered all over his face since you returned from Illinois, like I told you."

"Oh Sylvi, I've been so confused about everything, but it's wonderful now."

"I can't wait to see the gown you'll be wearing for the party. Where is it?"

"They are making final adjustments. For the price, they want a perfect fit. They'll deliver it tomorrow, I think."

"I'm just so glad all the craziness is over about Becky."

"Not entirely. There is always the chance the papers will get the whole story and Ellen finding out some of the worst details."

"Right, I'm concerned about it, too. He asked me to wait on telling her I'm her aunt until he gives the go ahead."

"Hopefully, soon."

"I agree."

CHAPTER TWENTY-ONE

Orchestral sounds from the music room drifted all the way to my room while Sylvi helped me dress. I was so nervous my hands shook while applying my makeup and I wanted it perfect.

"Will you stop squirming? I can't get the zipper . . . there," Sylvi said. "Wow, what a dress. People will talk about you for weeks."

"I feel like I'm going to burst over the top. It's not too revealing?"

"Not at all."

"Good. I wonder if MaryLou will be here?"

"Who?"

"At Ellen's party. Friends of Hugh's and their daughter were simply awful to me. Well, the wife was. Her husband seemed to be taken by me and the daughter bragged about her Christian Dior dress and snuggled up to Hugh. I thought they were . . . well, never mind, they weren't."

"Oh, them. I had the misfortune of being introduced. I hope they eat their words."

"Thanks Sylvi. It's such a relief to talk to you like a real bosom friend. You know how I hate secrets, and here I was having to keep a very big one. Is it this house or what?"

"Don't worry. We worked things out, and I am happy about it. I'd give you a big hug, but I don't want to ruin your fabulous hair and makeup. Earrings?"

"Yes, Hugh got them to go with the dress." I retrieved them off the dresser and clipped the S-design yellow pave diamond earrings set in yellow gold onto my ears.

"Wow, those look very expensive and they're perfect."

"I didn't ask how much. It's not ladylike, so I've been told when a man of means buys you a gift." I was giddy from the whole experience.

The two of us stood shoulder to shoulder in front of my full-length mirror, me in my white and gold gown pulling on white gloves and Sylvi in her green taffeta with her green gloves.

"Aren't we breathtaking?" I said.

"Sure are."

We giggled like schoolgirls.

"Ready?" She asked.

"Yep."

Jack and Hugh were waiting for us at the bottom of the stairs as we made our descent. Each of us took our man's extended arms, and we made our way through the crowd.

Hugh leaned in close. "Just as I expected, you look positively fabulous."

"And of course, so do you." I admired him in his black tuxedo. He really cut a fine figure, and he was all mine.

There weren't as many people at this party as at Ellen's birthday party, but still crowded. I laughed, because I didn't care how many came. My world revolved around Hugh and Ellen.

We went straight to the Music Room, or should I now say ballroom. All four chandeliers were brightly lit, filling the room with golden splendor. We joined the dancing couples on the parquet floor to the sound of the newest hit of 1953 "Till I Waltz Again with You" played by the ten-piece orchestra. The conductor wore a white-tuxedo waving his baton as he smiled at us. Did he know?

"Hugh, why didn't you have dancing at the other party? This is fabulous."

"Because it was Ellen's party, and she didn't want dancing. I gave her a choice."

"No kidding. I wonder what she'll want for her seventh. I may have to convince her of the dancing." I winked, and he held me close, twirling me around on the floor until the music stopped for a brief break and everyone applauded.

"Was Ellen difficult getting to bed?" Hugh asked.

"I explained why she couldn't be at this party. Didn't start until nine o'clock and she would already be asleep by then, anyway. I told her it was an adult thing."

"You have a wonderful way with her, Dee. She'll love having you for a mother." He squeezed my hand.

"I hope so. When are you doing the unveiling? I'm so glad Mr. Greene could finish repainting her portrait in time."

"They are sitting in the parlor behind a curtain. We'll move in there around ten-thirty."

Before the next dance, several of Hugh's business associates came up to talk to him, and they were all very gracious to me. It differed from the other party, or maybe I was different, more confident, and I clung to Hugh's arm like I belonged.

When the time came for the portrait unveiling, they ushered everyone into the parlor, where the two paintings sat on easels side by side.

When Hugh pulled the cord and the curtain opened, there was a thunderous applause and much inspecting of the paintings and congratulations from Hugh's business associates. The women were very interested in Ellen's portrait and asked about the artist. He couldn't attend and left plenty of business cards to hand out on his behalf.

"Hugh, are you going to have a second one done for the house?" I asked.

"No. I'm thinking all three of us together, as a family," he whispered in my ear.

A rush of love washed over my heart when he said family. I couldn't wait to tell Ellen when it was time.

When eleven-thirty rolled around, Hugh stopped the orchestra in the Music Room to get everyone's attention.

"May I have everyone's attention, please?" He shouted over the voices until they grew quiet. "Before we do the final countdown at midnight, I want to make a very special announcement."

He held his hand out and pulled me to stand next to him. Looking out across the crowd of expectant faces searching for judgments or frowns, finding none, I relaxed.

Hugh continued, "I would like to announce that Miss Deirdre Danes"—he paused for dramatic effect—"has accepted my proposal of marriage and we plan to be married this spring."

A surprising burst of applause filled the room, with a couple of cheers, though it might have been Jack and Sylvi. Guests surrounded us with congratulatory remarks and smiling faces. Even the Chabots came up to congratulate us.

"Well, well, aren't you the sly dog, congratulations," Jeeves said, shaking Hugh's hand.

There wasn't a snide remark from Martha, nor was she looking down her nose at me. "I'm thrilled for you, dear," she said.

"Miss Danes," MaryLou said, "I recognize your gown. I saw it at the Paris Fashion Week. Really suits you. Congratulations on catching a great guy, too." Her smile was sincere as she cast a longing look at Hugh.

He didn't even notice her. I think I gloated.

"Thank you MaryLou. I love yours, too."

Before we knew it, the final countdown began, and we welcomed 1954 into each other's arms.

The last guest was out the door as Hugh and I together bid farewells. The doorman shut the door and bid us a good night.

Jack and Sylvi came up behind us.

"Fantastic party," Jack said. "Best one I've ever attended."

"The first New Year's Eve party held here since my mother was alive," Hugh said.

"I didn't know. She loved parties, I've heard," I said.

"She did, and father did not."

"I'm not surprised." I shuddered at the thought of him.

"Well, we'll see you tomorrow," Jack said.

"I need to check in with the sitter we hired for tonight, to make sure Ellen actually slept," Sylvi said.

"I'll check in on her too when I walk this lady to her door," Hugh said. He pulled me into an embrace. "Did I kiss you at the strike of twelve?"

"Many times, thank you very much, and I could do with another."

"My pleasure."

CHAPTER TWENTY-TWO

January was in full swing when Hugh called me on the intercom. His tone was severe. I knew something had happened and hurried down to the library.

"Now what?" I worried at his serious face.

"My lawyers called me this morning. Becky has a lawyer in New York, where she murdered her husband. He's going for the insanity plea. They don't think they can keep it from the papers."

"There will be a trial after all? What would we do if Ellen heard her father was murdered and by someone who Ben and I knew? We can't keep her locked up in this house forever. She won't understand if you aren't the one to explain."

"Hoping the information doesn't go public. But I'm ready to tell Ellen." He took my hand and led me to the sofa. "I want you in the room when I tell her. She needs to know she has the two of us. I'll take all the responsibility for the secrets, but you will be her mother soon and—"

I put a finger to his lips. "Darling, you're right. We'll tell her together."

He kissed my hand and embraced me, gently kissing my lips. We melded together for a few breathless moments.

"When will you speak to her?"

"Now. Sylvi is bringing her down here."

"Now? Okay. That's good." Nervousness rose in me. "Will Sylvi be in on the discussion?"

"Yes, we have to tell Ellen who Sylvi really is and show her we are her family."

"I agree."

Sylvi came in with Ellen.

Hugh sat Ellen down on the sofa between him and me and Sylvi in the adjacent chair.

"Did I do something wrong?" Ellen said.

"No dearest," Hugh said. "We have something to tell you. Something it's time for you to know."

Ellen gave Hugh an expectant look.

He took a deep breath and held her little hand. "It wasn't until recently we learned that Nurse Clayton, uh, Sylvi, is your mother's sister. It's a wonderful surprise, don't you think? That makes her your aunt . . . Aunt Sylvi." He stopped to let it sink in.

Ellen was quietly thinking, looking at Sylvi, then back at Hugh. "Oh, I see." She furrowed her brow, then smiled. "That's good! I can call you Aunt Sylvi?" Then she frowned again. "But why didn't you know before?"

Hugh cleared his throat, and we all turned to him. "Well, turns out that your mother was my former wife, Nora, and . . . uh, we just figured it all out after she came to work here."

"You had a wife?" Ellen asked. "Then are you really my father?"

She didn't know about Nora, because no one could speak of her. My heart lunged for her confusion and wished there was something I could say, but the story was Hugh's.

"No, honey, your real father was someone else." He choked on the words.

I could tell he didn't want to tell that part of the story, and I didn't blame him. This was already a lot for Ellen to take in.

Sylvi chimed in. "Sweetheart. I had been looking for my sister for a long time. I didn't know about you. After I took this job, I found out that my sister had been married to your Uncle Hugh and . . . well, everything just came together. Are you happy that I'm your aunt?"

She told the story well, leaving out the facts that would further confuse Ellen or upset her.

"Yes, Aunt Sylvi. I think it's swell." Her face glowed.

"Now, Ellen," Hugh said, "this is a lot of information for you to understand, and there is a little more we need you to know."

Ellen quieted down to listen.

"You might hear some things said on tv or from your friends. It's something going on with a woman who says her husband was your real father."

"You told me my parents died in an accident."

"Sort of. You were too young to understand. But you are a big girl now and we can tell you. Your mother died shortly after you were born from an illness. I didn't know who your father was when I brought you here."

"Oh. How did he die?"

"Well, your father was married to someone else, not your mother. This other woman has just recently confessed to, uh . . . killing him."

I held my breath and I think Sylvi did too, waiting for Ellen's reaction.

"She killed him? Like in the movies?" The look on Ellen's face made me reach my hand out to her. She took it and squeezed hard.

"We don't know the details, honey," Hugh said.

That was true. We didn't know how Becky killed him or exactly when, either.

"Don't worry, the woman is in jail and they will put her away for a very long time for what she did." Hugh wrapped his arms about Ellen and hugged her, his hand covering mine and Ellen's.

Hugh relaxed back in his seat, heaving an enormous sigh. The weight he had carried for so many years had finally lifted. I could see the relief on his face. "Do you have questions?"

"So, my parents are still dead." She wrinkled up her face.

"That's right, honey," I said. "We just wanted you to know what we know, in case anyone asks you about it."

"What do I say?"

"You don't need to say anything to them if you don't want to," Hugh interjected. "Just tell them you don't want to talk about it. Can you do that?" Hugh looked worried again. I wanted to take his hand, but waited.

"Uh-huh," Ellen replied and nodded her head.

"That's a good girl. Any other questions?" Hugh said.

"Yes, Uncle . . . do I still call you Uncle Hugh?"

"An excellent question, Ellen," I said, giving an expectant glance at Hugh. He nodded, urging me to tell her. "Your Uncle Hugh and I are going to be married."

"Married?" Ellen's face lit up, and she bounced up and down on the sofa. "When? When?"

"In a few months. I am going to adopt you as my daughter."

"And I will adopt you as my daughter, too." Hugh said. Life had returned to his eyes, and they twinkled. "Do you know what adopting means?"

"I know someone who's adopted," said Ellen, "and she calls her parents mommy and daddy. Will I get to call you Mommy and Daddy too?"

I was smiling so hard, my mouth hurt. Hugh was beaming.

"It does pumpkin," he said.

"Oh boy! Aunt Sylvi, can I call your husband Uncle Jack?

"You sure can," Sylvi said.

"Gee, I have a whole family now."

"Yes, you do," Sylvi said.

We all laughed and smiled and hugged Ellen.

"Now remember Ellen, if you hear anything said or stories different from what we just told you, please come to any of us for answers," Hugh said.

"Okay."

My heart was so full of happiness, I thought it might burst.

***

Hugh went all out hiring extra staff to prepare for our wedding. Some days, I thought he was more excited about it than I. He wanted to share everything with me. Sylvi and Hugh stuck to me like glue during all the major decision-making activities. When we went to New York to shop for my wedding gown, we all went, including Ellen. I must admit it was wonderful to be surrounded by loving friends and soon to be family. Ellen behaved like a little lady the entire time and I was so proud of her as she helped to select her flower girl dress. I could tell she was fit to burst with excitement, though.

While I tried on the gowns, Hugh and Jack went to the menswear department to get fitted for cutaways and hats, gloves, the entire morning suit attire. Hugh had asked Jack to be the best man, since he was now officially Ellen's uncle.

The wedding was perfect. Three hundred people crowded into the garden and the first floor. Christian Dior designed my wedding dress, and a two-page spread in the Boston Globe covered the wedding and reception. I reveled in the experience, knowing it was going to be the one and only wedding I would ever have.

When Hugh and I departed Rothmorton for our honeymoon cruise to Europe, he turned to me in the back seat of the limousine.

"Dee, my darling, Dee. Thank you for coming into my life and making me whole again." He kissed me with such passion and love.

Breathless, I said, "You have filled the great void in my life. I guess we will thank each other for the rest of our lives." I giggled.

"Nothing would make me happier." And with that, he kissed me again, and again, and again . . .

ABOUT THE AUTHOR

An award-winning author, P. L. Jonas, has a creative spirit with a passion for literature, art, and music. She began writing fiction after a long career in marketing and technical writing and editing. A native Arizonan, she has traveled all over the U.S. and ten other countries. Drawing on her personal experience, a fascination with history, and a love of research, she weaves intricate stories of romance, sci-fi/fantasy, historical fiction, and suspense. In 2021, she received First Place in the Chanticleer International Book Awards, Goethe category, for late historical fiction. When not writing, she is reading or painting while her beloved cat looks on.

NOTE FROM THE AUTHOR

Word-of-mouth is crucial for any author to succeed. If you enjoyed *Hall of Deception*, please leave a review online—anywhere you are able. Even if it's just a sentence or two. It would make all the difference and would be very much appreciated.

Thanks!
P. L. Jonas

We hope you enjoyed reading this title from:

BLACK ROSE
writing™

www.blackrosewriting.com

Subscribe to our mailing list – *The Rosevine* – and receive **FREE** books, daily deals, and stay current with news about upcoming releases and our hottest authors.
Scan the QR code below to sign up.

Already a subscriber? Please accept a sincere thank you for being a fan of Black Rose Writing authors.

View other Black Rose Writing titles at www.blackrosewriting.com/books and use promo code **PRINT** to receive a **20% discount** when purchasing.

www.ingramcontent.com/pod-product-compliance
Lightning Source LLC
Chambersburg PA
CBHW030426120726
47903CB00003B/832